SECRETS ENEMY

SECRETS
ENEMY

RONALD HALE

S.I.T.E.
PUBLISHING

Copyright © 2023 by Ronald Hale

All rights reserved. Except as permitted in the U.S. Copyright Act of 1976, no part of this publication may be reproduced, distributed, or transmitted in any form or by any means, or stored in a database or retrieval system, without the prior written permission of the publisher.

ISBN: 979-8-9880626-0-8
LCCN:

This book is a work of fiction. Names, characters, places, and incidents are the product of the author's imagination or are used fictitiously. Any resemblance to actual events, locales, or persons, living or dead, is coincidental.

10 9 8 7 6 5 4 3 2 1

Printed in the United States of America

(Paperback) First Edition: April 2023

SITE PUBLISHING
7330 Staples Mill Road #106
Richmond, VA 23228

Ronald Hale
ronhalebooks.com
sitepublishingtoday@gmail.com

Cover Design: JenC Designs

New to the **SECRETS** series?

*Enjoy all **three** books in the trilogy:*

SECRETS END (Book 1)
When criminal attorney Todd Banks uncovers a secret from his past, he finds himself questioning everything and everyone he knows. As he struggles to disentangle himself from an ever-expanding web of lies and betrayal, Todd discovers just how much his past has dictated his present.

SECRETS BEGIN (Book 2)
Growing up on the tough streets of Boston, where poverty and crime are the norm, and the only way out is in a body bag, prison or a miracle, fourteen-year-old Khalil Gilliam's life is turned upside down when a family secret is revealed.

Years later, he meets Todd Banks, a successful Boston attorney who reveals the truth about the secret buried years ago.

SECRETS ENEMY (Book 3)
With their family secrets already exposed, Todd and Khalil believe they are finally in the clear… until Khalil learns the lies he and Todd uncovered go deeper than either of them ever believed.

As they strive to reveal the truth once and for all, they discover just how deeply the lies and deceit have infiltrated their inner circle. Not everyone who smiles at you is happy to see you.

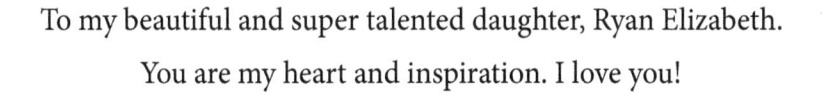

To my beautiful and super talented daughter, Ryan Elizabeth.
You are my heart and inspiration. I love you!

"Children are a blessing and a gift from the Lord."
Psalm 127:3

PART ONE

HUNTER

Chapter 1

TRUST UNCLE LEE to come barging in like that! Couldn't he see I was fast asleep, snoozing peacefully like a baby in a cradle? Nearly made me hit the ceiling with fright, he did, storming into the bedroom like a whirlwind. Or a herd of elephants. Or both.

Not so quietly, he stomped inside, making sure to slam the door hard at his back. As my sandbagged eyes slowly struggled to open, I could immediately sense his presence. Well, all the noise had kind of given it away, and in my mind's eye, I could see him standing there, one shoulder leaning against my closed door, wild eyes staring at me through the darkness.

Shifting around in bed and rubbing the gunk from my eyes, I heard a deep, wispy sigh escape from between his wrinkled lips. I knew that sound too.

"Rise and shine, soldier," Uncle Lee flatly said. "Time to get up. Can't stay there all day, you know, son. No one pays you to lounge in bed."

Huh? I thought. No one pays me at all! What's he going on about?

As usual, I didn't know a word he was talking about, but it never did shut him up, so I said nothing in retort because it was pointless. Humming a little tune to himself, one I didn't recognize, I heard him stroll across the room and open the window blinds right next to my bed.

Following that, an immediate flood of bright morning sun rushed in, washing all four walls in a stream of bright yellow light. Before I even had a chance to fully wake up, I was already struggling to see through the shimmering glare. He was trying to blind me! Then he flung the window open. Okay, so you're going to freeze me as well. Just great.

I pulled the comforter over my head to drown out the light. Just seconds later, the monotonous tone of my electric alarm clock began buzzing away on the bedside table.

"Rise and shine," Uncle Lee repeated. "Let's get up and about! UP and ABOUT!"

Where he got his energy, I'd never know. He was far too old for this kind of morning enthusiasm, only it appeared he hadn't noticed that fact. But it just wasn't natural.

And it also wasn't nice to have to suffer it. I moaned and groaned as usual.

With one hand, he reached over and silenced the repetitive squawk of my alarm.

"Today's the first day of the rest of your life, Hunter, son. Best get an early start on it, eh?"

I didn't want any start at all, let alone an early one. The fluffy covers of my bed were still coaxing me, and as yet, my brain was asleep. Eventually, he shuffled away, probably grumpy.

Hiding, I listened to the rhythm of his heavy footsteps as he moved back toward the bedroom door. "And don't forget to make every moment count. We live but once."

With that, he opened the door and silently walked out. Even then, I could still hear his crass statements as he wandered away down the landing toward the bathroom. "It's a wonderful life and I thank the Lord for every day. Praise God and praise our wonderful sun and nature too…"

Even with how annoyed and tired I was, I knew my uncle only wanted the best for me. I appreciated him especially since his career had taken a sudden turn for the worst, yet he was still trying his best for me, night and day. It was as if his life revolved around me, and I felt lucky.

Uncle Lee was a retired decorated Navy Seal who had proudly served his country for the better part of twenty-five years. Unfortunately, due to a deadly case of friendly fire that would ultimately claim the lives of three people in his squadron, Uncle Lee had been forced into an early retirement. Not only that, but he'd also been diagnosed with a severe case of PTSD. And with good reason. Needless to say, he was never the same after that awful tragedy in the field. Who would be? He put on a brave face every single day of the week, no matter what. It was hard not to love and respect any man who managed to do that, who also always put others first.

But despite him trying his hardest, it was clear that every day was a struggle for him. I knew it because I could see his pain written on his face, in his eyes, and sometimes, tears almost fell because the agony was that brutal no matter how hard he tried to keep it bottled up inside.

"Whatever you do," Uncle Lee would sometimes lecture, "don't ever let the hard things in life bring you down. Always try to stand on your own two feet. Most importantly, never—and I mean never—depend on anybody to make a living for you. It just ain't honest."

Choosing to forever internalize those words of wisdom, my right arm tugged the comforter from over my head and I reluctantly stared up at the slow spin of the ceiling fan. Hopefully, that even spiral would somehow pull me out of my unmotivated state. But of course, it didn't.

A few short minutes later, my wobbly legs had finally managed to crawl out of bed and scurry over to the bathroom. Time to start the daily morning routine.

Shortly, in the kitchen, Aunt Jane was already sitting at the table, reading the Boston Globe on her iPad. "Good morning, sweetie," she said without looking up. "Cheerios or Quaker Oats?"

"Nah, I'm good. Thanks."

Instead, a shiny red apple seemed to be beckoning from the overstocked fruit bowl in the center of the kitchen table. After polishing the fruit with a shirt sleeve, my mouth relished the juicy sensation of sinking in my teeth for a big bite—not that minty toothpaste and bitter apple really complemented one another, but it was too late. The deed was done.

A healthy breakfast in hand, my body spun around, those

same spindly legs kindly transporting me back to the bedroom as if programed to do it, every day the same.

The rest of that morning was spent idly scrolling through my phone, checking Instagram and Snapchat messages. Just like Aunt Jane, it was fair to say that social media was taking up a lot of my time these days. We were both a bit, well, addicted to it, you could say.

Since moving to Boston for Aunt Jane's new job a few months prior, it had quickly become my only means of entertainment. A much-needed escape. She must have found the same, though to be honest, wasn't she supposed to have a job that kept her a bit busier?

Aunt Jane was a high-profile attorney. From the bits she had related, what had brought her all this way to Bean Town was a high-profile insider trading case involving the CEO of some large corporation. She talked about it a lot—managing to always remind us she wasn't to mention it.

"Oh, it's confidential!" she'd say with pride. She loved that—always bringing it up so she could say she wasn't allowed to talk about it. Kind of dumb if you ask me.

But, after a couple minutes of awkward silence, she'd start telling us stuff anyway.

That's just how she was.

Anyway, on this morning, after the apple had been duly chomped, Aunt Jane and I crossed paths by the trash bin in the kitchen. She had me cornered now. Oddly, she was no longer distracted by her digital newspaper either, and for a change, her eyes were no longer magnetically attached to her device. She quietly sipped at her cup of coffee.

Then came her question, the one she'd obviously been brewing.

"So… are you ready for your first day of school, Hunter?" Her green eyes narrowed as she leaned against the painted door-frame, awaiting my response. Wasn't the answer obvious?

This was hardly scintillating conversation.

Sitting down in my usual spot at the kitchen table, I leaned back in my chair and passively shrugged and said the same thing any frustrated kid would say. "Dunno… Guess so."

It was hard to fake an interest, staring down at my phone, mindlessly sifting through an endless feed of pointless Instagram stories. Her eyes were burning into the top of my head.

"Well, you should have prepared for it," she went on. "This is your junior year, Hunter."

So, tell me something I don't know, my inner voice yelled. What is it with these grown-ups that they always have to boss a kid like me about? It's like some sort of sport! Aunt Jane gets the gold medal, Uncle Lee not far behind with the silver... Give me a break!

Although I wasn't looking at her, her hard stare was still pressing down on me, as if measuring my ability to grasp the situation. "Just remember, the world is your oyster."

More banal phrases. Between Uncle Lee and her, they seemed to know a whole encyclopedia of these stupid things. Besides, I never really understood what that one was supposed to mean.

The world is my oyster. Great. What if I'm allergic to shellfish?

It just so happened I was, too.

So, to use one of Uncle Lee's phrases this time, 'stuff that in your pipe and smoke it'.

Now, my stomach was wobbling, full of chuckles. And she didn't know what the laughing was for and glowered at me. "What on earth's wrong with you, Hunter? Don't you take anything seriously?" There was a brief lull from across the table before Aunt Jane cleared her throat and added, "Oh, and be sure to stay clear of those kids that can't help but spout their own political agendas. No need to go and get yourself mixed up in that reactionary nonsense."

"Ha, okay. Sure!" I laughed.

At the time, it seemed she was trying to be funny, so I smirkingly countered with, "I promise to only associate with jocks, cheerleaders, and kids who loudly support the Black Lives Matter movement. Scout's honor." Our eyes met. She wore a face like thunder. Whoops!

Passing by to rinse his empty coffee mug in the kitchen sink, Uncle Lee glanced over at us both and gruffly proclaimed, "Jesus didn't die up there on the cross for some. He died for all."

"Listen," Aunt Jane sighed, ignoring her husband as she rolled her emerald eyes up to the ceiling and back down. "What I mean is, please stay away from anyone supporting BLM. Those people have their own agenda, and it has nothing to do with equal rights. Trust me on that."

Confused, I set my phone down on the table and eyed her suspiciously. "Wait a minute… weren't you at the 'Get Your Knee Off Our Necks' march they had in Washington? I don't get it, that was clearly a protest against police violence. Isn't that pretty much the same thing?"

Aunt Jane shoved her chair back and stood up from the table.

With a rather sour expression on her face, she began collecting dishes. "All I have to say is, like those associated with BLM, I too have an agenda. But mine is valid."

"Agenda? A valid one?" I sneered, snatching another shiny red apple from the fruit bowl between us. "What agenda would that be?"

"Running for Attorney General of Massachusetts, that's what."

My eyes went wide. Really? That's what she was up to?

After stacking the used dishes in the kitchen sink, I watched as Aunt Jane snatched her briefcase from the hall closet, turning back to blow Uncle Lee a big kiss goodbye from the next room. To me, she simply smiled and winked. Her better disposition had made an appearance.

"Enough with the twenty questions already, Hunter. It's about time for you to head off to school, isn't it?"

Sadly, she was right.

Chapter 2

MAKING MY WAY through the crowded school hallway, an unfamiliar female voice called out from somewhere behind.

"Hey! Hey, kid! You lost or something?"

Unsure of where or who the voice was originating from, my fingers coyly slipped the school's welcome packet back into my open backpack. This was a lame attempt to blend in, to not stand out as the ignorant new kid. Turning on my heels, a mixed reaction of utter surprise and extreme intrigue passed over my face when our eyes finally met.

It was a girl, so stunning! How beautiful she looked.

Cutting through the passing crowd, my head was already swooning as she reached out and placed one hand on my shoulder, as if to help me keep my balance. For what felt like an eternity, we gazed into each other's eyes, neither one of us saying a word.

"Hi," the girl finally said, removing her soft touch from my arm. It was as if a sweet angel had momentarily touched me, and from now on, this school sweater would never be washed! Her scent—something like talcum powder and a light fragrance—lingered in my nostrils. Unfortunately, it made me want to sneeze and scurry away. My nose managed to behave itself.

Taking a few steps back, she extended her right hand forward for a formal handshake.

"My name's Destiny. And you are?"

"Hunter." My voice was barely above a whisper, hardly very masculine. I tried again, looking for something deeper this time. "Hhhunter," I growled, throaty, as if afflicted by a bad 'flu.

Raising the right hand to meet hers, everything around seemed to be moving in slow motion, giving all the time in the world to admire her big brown eyes and warm smile.

Softly, her button nose wrinkling in amusement, she tilted her head and asked, "You got a last name, Hunter?"

"Oh… yeah, it's James." Like a warm rush of water passing

over me, my confidence slowly began to filter back through. "Hunter James. That's me."

When the world started to speed back up again, it suddenly dawned on me that Destiny and I were still holding hands. At the same moment as my hand gently pulled away from hers, a tall, blond guy pushed me aside. As he did, he draped one twig-like arm around Destiny's narrow shoulders. "Yo, who's the new kid?" he inquired, causing my guts to knot and squirm.

"Oh, no one," Destiny said. At least, my ears told me she'd said it. My ego was too busy shrinking away to take a lot of notice of her comment. Though admittedly, it hurt.

Hopefully, it was a case of mishearing. Now, my ego puffed itself again, staring at him.

The boy scowled, not bothering to hide the fact that he was actively sizing me up too.

My fists were clenching at my sides as if possessing a mind of their own. Although we'd literally just met, a fresh spike of hateful anger was already starting to course through me.

That's right, keep on smilin', buddy, my mind was saying, both palms clammy with rage-laced sweat. Bet I could knock you out with one good punch if I really wanted to…

But the first day in a new school was hardly the time to go punching random kids in the face. Even if they did deserve it. My fists obeyed and unfurled as my brain said just ignore him.

For better or worse, I chose to take myself off in the opposite direction, walking away.

In front of a row of blue lockers, I stopped walking, intent on retrieving that welcome packet from my backpack. Suddenly, Destiny appeared out of nowhere and nestled up to my side. So, it's her again. She didn't stand up for me. So I'll ignore her, show her what's what!

Swallowing hard, I stiffly nodded and asked, "Hey. What's up? You okay?"

Oh. Oh dear. Well, it was hard to sideline such a pretty girl.

Face beaming with a smile, Destiny jokingly pouted. "That's very rude of you to have walked away without saying goodbye first. Don't you know that? I think you'll find it difficult to make friends with that kind of attitude, Hunter. I thought we were friends."

Huh. I don't think your boyfriend wants me hanging around you, I thought.

"No disrespect," I started to say, staring at her blankly, "but I'm not here to make friends. Not with you or that Machine Gun Kelly lookalike who pushed me. He's why I walked away."

Averting my eyes again to my open backpack, I added, "It was nice to meet you, Destiny, but I have to find where my homeroom is before the bell rings."

Flirtatiously, Destiny leaned forward and playfully whispered, "Oh, that's just Rick. Don't mind him. He likes to run his mouth a lot, but he's harmless. Besides, you need me!"

To this last bit, I couldn't help but chuckle.

"Oh, I need you, huh? What do I need you for?" It was clear now. Destiny was either crazy, incredibly confident, or a little bit of both. Who in their right mind just walked up to someone they didn't even know and said something like that? That was strange. The question was whether to entertain her faux friendliness or run for the nearest exit…

Either choice would come with serious consequences.

Welcome packet in hand, I tried to turn away from her, but it was too late. In a flash, Destiny slipped her arm under mine and held tight. With all the confidence of royalty, she began to lead me toward room 312, which strangely happened to be my assigned homeroom class.

"Today's your lucky day, Hunter," she cooed, clearly enjoying herself as she tugged me down the hallway like a toy on a string. "Because I'm going to be your personal chaperone."

Yeah, and continue to invade my personal space, I thought.

When she looked over to gauge my reaction, only a half-cocked smile came to me. "Thanks."

Seconds later, Destiny let go of my arm, grabbed my welcome packet from my hand, turned, and walked away.

Chapter 3

"I GOT A QUESTION for you, newbie," an unbelievably cute, blue-eyed blonde seated directly to the left of me turned to ask. Her angelic and curious face now only inches away from mine, she leaned across an open desk between us. When she was sure she had my attention, she cupped her hands around her bubble gum pink lips and whispered, "How do you know Destiny?"

Before I could even muster up half a response, my peripherals caught Destiny walking in through the classroom door, heading straight in my direction.

The stolen welcome packet was dangling from her right hand.

"I believe this is yours," she curtly said, dropping it on my desk as she approached. Without another word, she then sat down in the empty desk between me and the cute blonde girl, then faced the front of the class as if we were strangers again.

"Uh… thanks," my voice mumbled, unsure how to feel about the gesture. Finally, I waited until Destiny glanced back over at me to flash an appreciative smile. Smoothly, my lips parted, saying, "You know, I was about to send out a search party for my stolen welcome packet."

This offhand joke made Destiny giggle. "Oh, you got jokes now? Nice."

She leaned over and jabbed me in the arm with her stubby finger. "Well, Hunter, you may be exactly what this school's been missing."

"What do you mean by that?" the blue-eyed blonde suddenly asked. Before Destiny could outright dismiss her, the girl slid her chair closer and attempted to join in on the conversation.

Rolling her eyes in exasperation, Destiny leaned in, whispering, "Be sure to stay away from Harper here. She may look cute, but she's a bleached blonde bimbo who can't be trusted."

"Oh? Why's that?" Over Destiny's shoulder, my vision caught sight of Harper, staring at us with an expression of blank wonder.

"Take heed of my words, pretty boy," Destiny warned, thin eyebrows raised in amusement, "Harper is bad news. Just take my word for it. Or it's at your own peril."

As I mulled over this cryptic warning, Destiny took the opportunity to quickly stand up from her desk and leave the room. It wasn't until my eyes wandered back down to my own desk that I realized she'd made off with my envelope yet again.

What the hell's with this girl and my welcome packet?

None of this made any sense to me. Only to make the situation even more uncomfortable, I now had to avoid making eye contact with Harper, who glared at me, clearly pissed.

Not even a full minute passed by when I heard a gruff voice at my side. It was Harper, but this time, not in such a friendly mood anymore. Thin arms crossed tight over her budding chest, Harper gasped, "The next time you feel like talking smack about me behind my back to Destiny, or anyone else in this school, don't! Got it? Because if you do—"

That was when an overweight boy seated directly behind squealed with laughter and said, "Ha! There she goes again! Harper: the drama queen. Up to no good, as always."

Grabbing the water bottle from her desk, Harper leaped out of her seat, spun around, pulled off the bottle cap, and squirted the boy right in the face.

"What the hell, Harper!" the boy shouted, puffy face and shirt now drenched in beads of water as he stumbled up from his desk. By this time, everyone was laughing at the stunt, some even recording the funny incident on their phones and uploading it to their social media.

"Sit your huge fat butt down there before I totally end you," Harper gravely warned, threatening the boy with the last few squirts left in the bottle. But instead of following through, she turned and pointed it directly at me. Me? Why me? What've I done?

Offered no time to react, I looked straight down the barrel of the bottle as Harper squeezed out the remaining squirt right into my big dumb face. The whole classroom erupting in unhinged laughter for the second time, my body seemed to be just sitting there, cold water rolling down my brow and chin. Boy, did I feel stupid. And look stupid.

What a way to start my first day of school, I thought, more embarrassed than angry.

Seconds later, in walked a short-haired brunette woman wearing a fitted blue and white sweatsuit. Confidently, she crossed the room to stand at the front of the class.

"Good morning, everyone," she pleasantly said, flashing her pearly whites as she spoke. Her voice was authoritative, yet calm and enduring—like a mother addressing her own children. Patiently, her cool eyes watching over the room, she waited for the other students to take their seats before continuing, "For those of you who don't already know, I'm Mrs. Davis. I will be your homeroom teacher this year. Fun fact about me: I'm also the school's physical education teacher and girls' varsity basketball coach."

During the formal introduction, Mrs. Davis turned her back to the class to jot her name down on the blackboard in big block lettering—even larger than the embroidered lettering of the school name splashed across the back of her track jacket.

"Uhm, we're not blind, Mrs. Davis," a kid in the back row called out, half joking.

Taking a seat at her desk, Mrs. Davis carefully scanned the crowded room. Unexpectedly, her eyes caught mine and stayed there. "Are you Hunter James?"

Her loud voice forced everyone in the room to focus on me, of course.

"Yes, ma'am," I responded, making sure my tone was

respectful and not condescending like the last boy. Something told me it would be wise not to cross her in such a way.

Or else.

"Welcome to Cloud Valley High School," she said with a cordial smile. "Home to the city's champion girls' basketball team." To the class now, she raised her voice and added, "Everyone, please join me in welcoming Hunter to our humble abode."

Humble abode. Pfft, that's rich…

Reminiscing on my morning spent being hounded by a total kleptomaniac, it was hard not to let my disdain show. Aside from Destiny stealing my belongings not once, but twice, there was still the counterfeit Machine Gun Kelly to think about, Rick. Whoever he was, he hadn't seen the last of me, that was for sure. And finally, there was the water bottle assassin, Harper.

If this is what these people consider hospitality, I can't wait to see what their school pride looks like.

Why had I gone in that day expecting to be greeted with open arms and smiling faces?

I guessed in a way, I'd just got exactly what was deserved for making such a stupid assumption in the first place. Served me right. "Thanks," I finally echoed back to the class.

Slowly, I slid down low in my seat, waiting for the merciful sound of that first period bell. But before I knew it, the class's focus was on me once again.

"Wait a minute," Mrs. Davis said, perking up from her desk. Swiftly, she moved through the aisles to where I sat, her eyes gleaming with hopeful recognition. Standing at my side, she studied my face for a few moments before hesitantly asking, "Were you… I mean… are you familiar with Central City Academy in Peoria, Illinois?"

"Yes, ma'am," I answered.

"No way," she gasped, scurrying back over to her desk to retrieve her cell phone. Once back at my side, she held the phone out, bluntly asking, "Is… is this you, by chance?"

Thankfully, the first period bell rang.

Chapter 4

WITHOUT HESITATION, I leaned forward, grabbed my backpack from the floor, and made a mad dash for the exit. Linger around this place long enough, and I'd end up being the unwilling participant in a game of twenty-one questions. In any case, there was some hunting to do, to track down the thief who'd taken off with my belongings. It was my one and only welcome pack, and without that, there'd be no way of avoiding getting into trouble. It wasn't good to be late for my first period class—especially on the first day of school!

Great. Thanks a lot, Destiny, I bitterly thought. What is it about my stuff that's so interesting to you anyway?

Like a wandering zombie, I weaved my way through the crowded hallway looking for her, but to no avail. Just when things couldn't get any worse, heads began to turn in my direction. It was Harper again, heading straight for me—as focused as a homing missile.

Clearly, she'd fixed on her target.

"Hey, green eyes!" Harper boisterously shouted. When our paths finally collided in the busy hallway, she threw her arms up around my neck, forcing the front of her body against mine. "Do you forgive me for squirting you earlier? Oh, please say yes. I really like you, you know!"

Shrink… cringe…

Even with the sudden apology and the short time since we'd met, I knew Harper better than that. This girl was bent on assault. But no matter her true intentions, no way was she gonna squirt me a second time! Continuing to stand with Harper in the middle of the hall, being awkwardly groped against my will, a hard hand slap landed on my right shoulder.

Twirling on my heels to face away from a clingy Harper, I faced the new presence, immediately blushing. There he was, Machine Gun Kelly who'd assaulted me earlier.

"What's up?" I managed to say, instinctively clenching my fists.

In that moment, a raw surge of adrenaline rushed through me, an inner geyser of savage impulse. If it came to it, I was ready to fight. For several long seconds we stood motionless, facing each other like two rugged cowboys about to have a showdown, our eyes unflinching.

But just as I thought we might stare at each other for an eternity, he stretched out his hand.

Huh? Now, he's confusing me.

With a cunning smile dancing across his lips, he said, "Welcome to Cloud Valley. Gotta say, I look forward to winning the state championship with you later this year."

A sigh of relief escaped. A full-on fist fight hadn't broken out, so I reluctantly shook hands.

"You still haven't answered my question," Harper buzzed in my ear, her voice akin to that of a persistent bumble bee. She pressed her body against mine, front to front, so close that I could feel her heartbeat as her chest pressed into mine.

In an instant, my teenage hormones reacted the only way they knew how.

And, boy, did people notice.

"Look! The new kid's got a boner!" a tall girl standing a few feet away yelled, pointing wildly down to the enlarged crotch of my pants. As everyone turned and looked, I tried to turn away, but it was useless. Surrounded on all sides, there was no escape from the inevitable. And as much as I wanted to pretend my body hadn't betrayed me in the worst possible way, there was no escaping it. The damage had already been done.

"Oh my," Harper gasped, stepping back toward the crowd. "Did I do that?"

A sinking feeling of intense panic swept over me then. Face so hot that it could fry an egg, I covered my crotch with my backpack, quickly parting the crowd. Ignoring the teasing and jeering from my classmates, I headed straight for the bathroom and quickly retreated inside.

"Ah, crap! This can't be happening right now!" My voice echoed off the white tiling and into oblivion. Suddenly, the bathroom door opened at my back. Still covering myself, my body turned. The fat kid from homeroom class came waltzing in.

"Don't feel bad," he said. Casually, he approached one of the long rows of porcelain sinks and turned on the faucet. I remained there, watching a stream of discolored water splash into the cracked sink bowl. "Harper has that kind of effect on people. You'll get used to it."

I sighed. "I, yeah… I noticed…" Finally able to control my bodily functions again, I gathered my backpack and exited the bathroom, fully prepared to face the firing squad, but back outside in the hallway, only Destiny was waiting for me.

Of course, she had my worn welcome packet pinched in her right hand.

"There he is! Mr. Hunter James," she teased, looking me up and down as she spoke. "I've been looking for you."

I bet you were. Shades of red were still lingering in the hollows of my pale cheeks. Too bad you didn't find me a little sooner. Maybe then, all that crap could've been avoided.

Destiny must've sensed something had happened; she flashed a puzzled look.

"Are you okay? You seem upset."

A nervous laugh came. "It's… uh… well, never mind. No, really, I'm okay."

Not wanting to relive that embarrassing moment all over again, it was better to change the subject. "So, where to now?"

"Chemistry."

Destiny handed over my welcome packet for the second time, my hand managing to deftly slip it inside my backpack for safekeeping. No way would she get to snatch it away for a third time. Not on my watch. Walking back down the hallway, I purposely trailed a few steps behind, quietly watching her hips sashay as she walked.

Within minutes, we had arrived at my chemistry class.

"I guess this is the place, then." I was trying to drag out the moment, not wanting our time together to end. Stop being so corny, Hunter. It's ridiculous.

Besides, we weren't on a date or anything. Not yet anyway.

"I guess so." Destiny sighed. Was she feeling the same way? But that didn't matter. Smiling, she laid a heavy wink on me and said, "All right, well, good luck, Hunter! See ya around!"

She reached about halfway down the hall.

"Destiny! Wait!"

"Yes, Hunter?" Her brown eyes narrowed as she turned and gazed back at me. I could feel myself getting lost in those eyes, sinking in them like two pits of glittery quicksand.

"Thank you for taking the time to make me feel welcome today." A shy smile traversed my face. "And if it's okay, I'd like to return the favor."

Looking around, Destiny made sure the coast was clear before waving me back over. Quickly, I jogged up the short length of hallway and faced her. "Really? Do you mean it?"

Nervously, I heaved my backpack on my shoulders, trying hard to meet Destiny's open stare.

Now or never, man. The courage had to come. Better to face rejection now than miss your only opportunity to ask her out. Go! Hurry up and do it now or you'll chicken out!

"I don't mean to sound too forward…" A deep shade of hot red was rising in my face again. "Any chance of getting your number? No big deal if you don't want to give it to me, though…"

My heart clenched. Destiny's brow immediately creased at the sensitive question. "My number? You want my phone number?"

With a slight frown, she folded her arms. "What do you want my phone number for, Hunter?"

"I was thinking that… well… we'd hang out after school sometime. If you want to…"

The worst had happened; I'd put myself out there, winning back just a hardened stare. The boner incident with Harper had been bad, but this felt so much worse, like being the main attraction in some traveling carnival freak show.

Was she just going to stand there and glare at me until I got cold feet and walked away? But a small smile played at the corner of her frowning lips. "First impressions are everything, you know?" she said, bright eyes still penetrating my insecure thoughts. "And not to be rude or anything, but we didn't exactly hit it off back there. Did we?"

That was it, game over. An official rejection. Strike three, you're outta here!

To save myself from any further embarrassment, I mumbled an incoherent thank you, spun away, and headed back to class, in that moment the loneliest boy on Earth.

As I reached one hand out for the classroom door, Destiny's voice called out behind me.

Wide smile blooming across her perfect face, she gave me another hard wink and yelled, "Hunter! Check your welcome packet!"

With that, she ran for an adjacent hallway and disappeared.

Chapter 5

NEEDLESS TO SAY, suffering through a long and arduous school day like that would be enough for anyone to throw in the towel. I'd had more than enough before we even began!

No, thanks. Hard pass!

But now that my secret was out to everybody at Cloud Valley High school, life would never be the same. By the end of that first day, it felt as though I'd never stood a fighting chance of just being another run-of-the-mill student who could disappear into the proverbial woodwork and not get himself noticed. No, the cards had always been stacked up against me, even when trying to be low-key and not make waves. Honestly, the day couldn't have gone any worse.

Well, it probably could, actually. It always can when I'm around.

So much for flying under the radar...

Making my way down the hall toward the school's front exit, I tried desperately to avoid everyone else around me. The last thing I wanted was more unsolicited attention. Any of it. But somehow, it was always possible to do something that made me forget my own promise to not draw attention. Suddenly, there were Destiny and Harper standing at the far end of a long row of closed lockers, feverishly whispering to one another. There was an urge to know what they were swapping notes about. Ah, but there was an equal desire to run and get the hell out.

If I'm quick, I can slip through the crowd for the back exit...

But just then, right before turning on my heels and high tailing it in the opposite direction, they both stopped talking and looked over. Silence fell as if the whole world had ended! Well, my world! Yup, you guessed it. My cover was blown. Or rather, I'd blown it. Again.

Now, they were standing gaping at me, rigid, nothing to say. Harper raised a hand, jabbing it in my direction. Destiny… well, I could swear I saw her snicker behind her hand.

But no, it couldn't be. Wasn't possible because they were both so quiet. Motionless.

That got me thinking. What're they being so quiet for? Seems kinda weird. Wait… why are they pointing at me like that? Oh crap, this can't be good…

Sensing more trouble on the horizon, my already hurried pace scuttled for the nearest exit. If this had been a cartoon, you'd have seen my little legs whizzing around, so fast you could barely see them, like a bicycle wheel. It didn't feel like a cartoon. It felt real. My ego was embarrassed.

But naturally, I was curious as to what Destiny and Harper were talking about, but not all that much. Whatever those two were discussing probably wasn't good for me to know.

Besides, I didn't really want to stick around and find out.

More than anything, there was a deep need to just get home and avoid any further craziness. That's it. I'd had my fill for one day. No such luck, however. Just as I was about to shove myself through the swinging front door and make my great escape, Destiny and Harper pounced.

SECRETS ENEMY

Like the last lonely chicken trapped in the hen house by hungry wolves, they'd cornered me.

"Hey, Hunter," Harper gruffly whispered. Although giving the illusion of speaking intimately, her words were more than loud enough to turn heads. One by one, the other kids stopped walking to casually observe our close-knit conversation. They stood around, the way a crowd waits for a fight to start. Hopefully, it wouldn't be that. Fighting girls was not manly!

"Where you off to in such a hurry? Hmm?"

"Uhm… uh… nowhere," came a fumbled response, right away, sensing something was up. Face frowning, again doing its own thing, my eyes rolled. "Why do you ask?"

Destiny spoke next. Not with a question, but a flat-out demand. "Hey, let me see your welcome packet again. Just for a sec." She knew just as well as I did what was inside that packet, maybe even better. To me, it looked as if she just wanted to play another game of keep away.

Well, not this time. Just this once, some sort of sense kicked in. Self-preservation.

Choosing to ignore her, my feet quickly pivoted away the girls' trap and bolted the last few inches for the door. Taking my first step on the other side, bright afternoon sunshine instantly warming my skin, my weight was at least a hundred pounds lighter, all stress floating away.

You did it, Hunter! You said no. Walked away. Go, you!

All the drama of the day lifted from my shoulders. Finally, my grueling eight-hour torture session was ending. And not a second too soon. Scanning the school's crowded front lot, I spotted Aunt Jane's car idling on the far side of the bus lane. It was like seeing a birthday cake.

I loved Aunt Jane so much right then in that moment. Aunt Jane. Rescuer…

One by one, a row of big yellow buses started their engines. These were the buses that came to take the other kids home, the ones who didn't have birthday aunties waiting. Not that it was my birthday or anything but—you get the gist. My heart leaped. She represented an escape.

Squinting through the heavy glare of afternoon sunshine, I took a deep breath of diesel-misted air. Ah, such bliss! All right, you got this. Only about fifty feet between here and Aunt Jane's car, and you're home free. Easy-peasy. You can do this, Hunter! Go for it! Now!

Unsurprisingly, about halfway across the front lawn, a shriek beckoned from behind.

"Hunter! Hunter, wait!" Stopped dead in my tracks, there

was no choice but to turn back and look. Sure enough, there were Destiny and Harper, holding hands. They cut their way through the waiting groups of dismissed teachers and students. Once the evil duo reached where I stood on the short island of clean-cut grass, Destiny took a moment to catch her breath.

These two are pursuing me! Like, actively giving chase! What the...?

"Why so secretive, Hunter? Why didn't you tell us everything from the beginning?"

Tell them everything? What are they on about now? What sort of 'everything'?

"Yeah, Hunter," Harper mockingly butted in. Eyes sharp and scrutinizing, she paused to brush a stray lock of hair from her smoothed brow. Slowly, she then traced the delicate angle of her jaw with her finger, her cherry red lips creased into a knowing smile. "Well, the cat's out of the bag now, so you might as well fess up already. Come on. Out with it."

Out with what? I had no clue. Really didn't.

"Look, will you two please just leave me alone," I frustratedly grunted, trying hard not to let that low boil of seething anger get the better of me. Not today. The two had put me through enough already. It was time to call it quits and head home.

But no matter how hard my words tried to convey this to them, they ultimately fell on deaf ears. This pair wasn't hearing it.

"Tell us now, or else," Harper further pressed, only half joking. "And don't leave out any details either. We want the whole story."

It was impossible not to laugh.

"Jesus, you two really are coo-coo for Cocoa Puffs, aren't you?"

Seriously, I'd had enough of their silly little games. With utmost conviction, I took a deep breath inward and leaned in close, making sure to speak nice and slow so both of them could hear me clearly over the guttural rumble of moving school buses. "Listen… if you two don't get out of my face, I swear to God I'm gonna—"

"You're gonna what, Hunter?" Harper boldly teased. "Gonna set Momma on us, right?"

"'Momma' isn't here, so no. That's my Aunt Jane. There, in the car. And yes, she'll sort you out." It sounded unduly aggressive. Unsure if they were teasing or really having a go at me, my ego was in the way again. This situation had to be defused. Besides, no way would Aunt Jane help me. She had her nose down toward her lap again, no doubt immersed in Facebook.

Without breaking her icy stare, Harper reached down to pull a small bottle of clear liquid from her open purse. Pointing the nozzle directly at my face, she scowled. "Go on! Try me!"

To this odd bit of dramatics, my head was shaking in disbelief.

"You have to be kidding. You do know you're the devil, right?" I laughed. Turning slightly, the threat had now been mitigated. She surely wouldn't attack a boy who wasn't even looking or willing to engage in battle! Now, I was facing an obviously amused Destiny. "What's with you guys? Why can't you just leave me alone already? I haven't done anything to you."

Instead of answering, Destiny coolly smiled and said, "Just tell us if the rumors are true. Well... are they? Please, just tell us."

The rumors? Oh God. This sounds so bad. No, worse than bad.

Beyond frustrated, teeth gritting and fists clenching, even they could tell the end of my rope was nearing. "I... I don't know how else to get this through to you two that I don't know what you're talking about! Okay? Stop bugging me about it!"

Just as my frustration was about to completely boil over, Aunt Jane exited her car, totally unaware that she was heading straight into this brewing storm of petty high school drama. As she slowly made her way across the parking lot, both my hands went up in the air..

"So… for the last time… I don't know what the hell you're talking about!"

Like a toddler on a trampoline, Harper giddily bounced in place as she wheezed, "Ha! Look at his face! I knew it! He's lying! He's lying! Look at him! It's so obvious."

Heart slamming in my chest like a pissed-off orangutang, I faltered to say anything, instead spitefully staring down at their smug, grinning faces. Did Harper tell Destiny about my embarrassing hallway boner moment? Is that what this is all about? An ill-timed woody? I mean, what else could it be? Man, I just don't know…

Racking my brain, a random group of kids suddenly stepped onto the lawn to join in the fun.

"What's goin' on over here?" a short, freckled-faced girl with long pigtails asked. Clutching the straps of her overstuffed backpack, she eyed all three of us with a healthy dose of curious skepticism. "What you yellin' for?" Her English was atrocious, though somehow, I managed to resist correcting her. Grammar was one thing my aunt and uncle were red hot on.

Her words jarred, but did I really want to challenge this freckle-faced ninny?

Begrudgingly, my fists went back down to my sides, head feebly shaking.

Once I'd managed to strip the anger from my voice, I responded, "For the last time, nothing's going on. It's literally nothing… Not that I know of, anyway."

With Aunt Jane slowly drawing near, there was no other choice but to exercise my Fifth Amendment right. The right to stay silent. Grabbing Destiny by the shoulders, I made her look me dead in the eye, then held my gaze there. "Look, I don't know what everyone's saying about me behind my back. Honest. Can we just talk about all this later? Please? I have to go."

It took her a moment to mull over the proposition, but once she did, a look of mild content washed over her face. "All right, it's a deal. Just make sure you call me before ten, okay?"

"You got it!" Like a man on fire, I darted away from the group just in time to intercept Aunt Jane as she stepped up onto the front lawn. Concerned, she saw the lingering lines of panic still on my face, clutched her car keys, and asked, "Is everything okay over here, Hunter? Are you all right?" As we continued across the busy parking lot for the car, she managed to glance back over her right shoulder at the loose group of wayward kids still pointing my way and giggling.

Even Aunt Jane could tell something was amiss.

"Yeah, everything's fine." The words shot out like a bullet from a gun. No way did I want to explain what was going on back there because, simply, I had no clue!

Only when reaching the car, pulling the front passenger door open, and climbing inside could a long sigh of relief finally come. "Whew!"

Aunt Jane looked askance at me. "You realize there's something weird about you today?"

"Yeah."

But thank Christ Almighty, the school day was officially over.

As I buckled my seatbelt and waited for Aunt Jane to pull away from the school, the Apple CarPlay dashboard suddenly lit up. She was getting a phone call from a name I didn't recognize. Right off the bat, this struck me as kinda odd.

Slowly, I turned in my seat. "Who's Todd Banks?"

Chapter 6

THAT AFTERNOON WHEN we arrived home, Uncle Lee was lounging on the couch in the living room. Feet hitched up on the chaise lounge, he had a cold beer in one hand while SportsCenter blared on the TV. Clearly, he was in his element, just living his best life.

Aunt Jane poked her head in just long enough to blow Uncle Lee one of her Hollywood kisses. Without missing a step, she made a hard beeline down the hall for the kitchen. There, she intended to wrap up her phone call with the mysterious Todd Banks.

Me? I had other plans.

Plopping down on the couch next to Uncle Lee, I playfully elbowed him in the ribs. "What up, Unc? You good?"

Despite managing a small conversational smile, my words felt profoundly heavy, not at all like a kid who'd just got home from school, and more like a middle-aged man just off a twelve-hour shift busting his ass down at the coal mines. All used up and dead to the world.

Leaning forward, I snatched the TV remote from the coffee table and began flipping through my personalized list of recorded episodes. All American was a real favorite of mine and Uncle Lee wouldn't mind watching it; he was constantly bragging about how great of a football player he used to be back in high school. "In my glory days," he often phrased it. "Way back…"

"So," Uncle Lee muttered in between a few hard swigs of beer. "Did you get to meet any pretty girls today? It's okay; you can tell me." He capped the last part with a not-so subtle wink from across the couch. A 'just between men' kind of thing.

"Well…" The words wouldn't come. "There's this one girl but I don't think it's—"

But before I could say any more about Destiny, Aunt Jane popped her head back in.

"Don't listen to your uncle, Hunter. School's about improving your social and educational skills. Preparing you for adulthood. Above all else, school's certainly not for meeting girls."

At the time, it wasn't clear why Uncle Lee's comment irked my aunt so much. It was as if she couldn't stand to hear any kind of dissenting opinion whatsoever, even from her own family. Didn't matter what the topic was. If you didn't agree with her, then you were wrong.

She was the embodiment of my way or the highway.

Simple as that.

"I just asked the boy if he'd met any pretty girls at school today," Uncle Lee fired back. "Jesus, Jane, you act like I asked him if he got laid in the hallway in between class. Chill out a little, huh? Other people are allowed to speak around here."

Even as Aunt Jane fully charged her way into the living room, Uncle Lee couldn't help but chuckle a little at the idea he'd just cast out into the atmosphere.

Frowning intensely, hands pitched on her hips, Aunt Jane was pissed, in full attack mode now. Not just ready for a fight, but hungry for one too.

Defiantly, she stood right in front of the TV screen, her face in the kind of snarling face a bulldog would make. "Well, unlike you, Hunter isn't about that kind of life. Besides, the last thing this society needs is another lazy man being catered to by a hard-working woman. God knows we got enough of that already."

The implication wasn't lost on ol' Uncle Lee.

Rising from his side of the couch, he quickly killed the rest of his beer—the whole time staring over the rim at Aunt Jane's hateful expression. He continued to eye her in this way as he dropped the empty beer can onto the coffee table between them.

This move only meant one thing.

Challenge accepted.

"What the hell's that supposed to mean? Taking care of another lazy man? Huh?" As Uncle Lee spoke, he tried to exude an air of controlled calmness. Deadly serious, but not at all perturbed. But underneath, he was genuinely offended by the remark. And who wouldn't be? Before Aunt Jane could muster up another sharp response, Uncle Lee let out a loud burp and headed into the kitchen for another beer. Less than a minute later, he was back at my side on the couch, almost draining his newly opened beer in one long swig.

This only further infuriated Aunt Jane.

She rolled her eyes, something that seemed habitual with her these days. "Should I spell it out for you then? Dammit, Lee, you know exactly what I meant…"

An achingly long stint of silence immediately followed.

They had stuck me in the middle of an emotional Mexican standoff, unable to move or speak in fear of making the already tense situation that much worse.

All I could do now was sit there and wait out the carnage.

Finally, after what felt like an eternity, Aunt Jane lowered her hard stare to the floor. But only for a moment. When their eyes met again, she whispered with teary eyes, "It's not my fault, Lee. You're… you're just not the man you used to be." Eyes still locked on his, she added, "Maybe if you'd stop feeling sorry for yourself all the time and cut back on the drinking, this poor excuse for a marriage would mean something to you. I mean… Christ, Lee, you used to be a man who commanded honor and respect. But now look at you, turning into a drunk loser. A bum."

He raised his eyes, shock reflecting in the shine of them.

She lessened the blow, perhaps knowing there'd be no coming back from what she had uttered. "Look, I didn't say you were a bum or a drunken loser. I said, turning into one. Please, Lee, don't go that way. You were always an upright man. A winner. A Navy man."

There. She had convinced the jury and now, she'd be the victor over the judge too. She knew how to say what needed saying, then to wind it back to a point where Uncle Lee could forgive.

But God knew, even now, what she had said—the truths revealed—were harsh ones.

From where I sat at my end of the couch, Uncle Lee's hard expression seemed to be dissolving in real time, that smooth transition from cool collectiveness to searing anger to saddened realization playing out right before my eyes. She had him. He was in torment.

It was all happening within a matter of seconds.

As Aunt Jane's hateful words fully absorbed into Uncle Lee's mind, I quietly watched as a single tear escaped his eye, a perfect droplet of warm saltwater traveling down the hollow of his cheek. This was the first time I'd ever seen my uncle cry. Ever.

Seeing him sitting there, a mask of suffering drastically aging his usually handsome face, was something I would never be able to unsee.

Then, the overwhelming urge came to say something. Anything.

"Stop talking to him like that!"

Just like poor Uncle Lee, a well of tears was now clouding my own sight. "Cut him a break already! You're supposed to be his wife! How can you go from blowing him kisses to this?"

Well, my brain sought to answer my own question: the kisses thing must be all a sham. Just put on, affected, acted out because this was how couples were supposed to act toward each other.

Vision swimming under a lens of watery tears, I blindly grabbed my backpack from the floor, threw myself from the couch, and stormed out.

Next came the thunderous BOOM! of my bedroom door slamming shut.

Conversation over. She'd surely learned a lesson from my words. Surely to God…

Sitting on my bed, headphones cranked to drown out any outside noise, I closed my eyes and tried to disappear. At some point, sleep must have come along to claim me because when I opened my eyes again and removed my headphones, the house was dead quiet.

Too quiet. Not a single sound to be heard from beyond that closed door.

For goodness' sake… surely not! Have they gone? Abandoned ship? Oh God, no!

Slowly, I got up from my bed to investigate. Thankfully, they had not evacuated the house and left me to fend for myself, to pay the wretched bills and everything, making me take a horrid ill-paid after-school job in some greasy burger joint! My heart could stop its drumming.

No, Aunt Jane turned out to be in the kitchen preparing dinner. Luckily, I snuck by unnoticed while her back was turned at the stove. On pins and needles, I headed farther down the hall to check on Uncle Lee in his room. Yes, I say his room because now, it came to my notice they hadn't been sleeping together either. Not for a while, in fact. They had their own rooms.

It was only now, what with the arguments, that this warranted any thought at all.

His door was open just a crack, barely enough to get a narrow look inside. Not sure what to expect, I cautiously knelt forward and took a peek.

Through the tiny crack in the door, a sad sight greeted my eyes. Uncle Lee lay sprawled out on his back across the bed. Face clenched in emotion, a demeanor appearing as hopeless as I had ever seen in a man, he openly gazed up at the ceiling. Then, he began to pray.

"Lord… I know, physically, I'm nothing like the man I used to be… Forgive me for the many sins that have brought me to this place, this shambolic lifestyle in which I immerse myself…"

His voice was so full of despair, a bad mix of extreme bitterness and repressed irritation. "I only ask that… well… that you find it within yourself to show me some mercy. Please, your

Holy Spirit, come fill this place with joy again… Come show me the way, I pray to you."

Continuing to kneel by the doorway, listening intently to his prayer and letting the odd tear slide down my pallid cheek, there came a sudden sound. Footsteps approaching.

The sound emanated from down the hallway's end.

"Hunter!" Aunt Jane shouted from the kitchen doorway, not crossing its threshold. "Tell your uncle that dinner's ready! Come and get it while it's still hot."

Why couldn't she be bothered to tell him herself? Had she now rendered her nephew the go-between? Well if so, that was pathetic! Whenever we kids argued, adults like Aunt Jane would be fast to tell us how stupid it was and that we shouldn't play silly games like refusing to speak to one another. We weren't supposed to be what she termed petulant—whatever that meant. And here she was, ignoring poor Uncle Lee, even in his direst hour of need. That was plain nasty.

Still crouched behind the partially closed door, I cleared the tension from my throat.

"Dinner's ready, Unc. You comin'?"

Through that same sliver in the doorway, I watched as he lazily turned on his back, his tear-stained face now facing me. With bated breath, he quietly answered, "Yeah. I'll be right there…"

Chapter 7

AFTER AN UNEVENTFUL dinner, Uncle Lee threw his dirty dishes in the sink and quickly ventured down to the basement to work out. Not a lot of conversation was had at the dinner table. Mostly, we just cleaned our plates and went about our business, each of us immersed in stony silence as if we weren't aware of sitting opposite anyone else. Awkward.

It was worse for me, caught between the pair of them. My mind constantly urged, tell them they're petulant! Go on, Hunter! Tell them! Tell them they're behaving like a pair of little kids!

I didn't dare. The wrath of Aunt Jane when she was in this kind of a stinking mood—well, it wasn't worth provoking. Who knew what she'd do? Or who knew what I'd imagine she'd do?

There'd even been one night ages ago, when she'd railed at Uncle Lee so much that in the night, I dreamed of her grabbing a long carving knife and stab, stab, stab! No kidding! Then she'd carved him right up like a turkey, cooked him, and embellished him with peas and beans!

My body shuddered at the reminiscence. Definitely didn't want to provoke anything that took me back to that awful place in my dreams. In fact, dreamland was where I felt at my best. Just drifting away, peaceful, no harassment from Uncle or Aunt, annoying freckly girls or teachers.

Needless to say, Aunt Jane was back on the phone with this Todd Banks guy—and I still didn't know who he was—right after dinner was over. They were discussing the details of her case, a real snooze-fest that I didn't care to overhear. It didn't even matter who this Todd was now. So, wanting to be alone, I headed to the back patio to organize my school binders.

At least out there in the cool night air, it would be possible to separate myself from the invisible fog of distress still lingering throughout the house, creating a cloying atmosphere. Some days when it got like this, it seemed hard to breathe, and the weakness in me wanted to cry.

Sitting on the back patio, carefully separating the syllabi for each individual course, I stumbled across that stupid thing—that annoying thing. Yes, my welcome packet. On the inside cover, written in blue ink, was Destiny's phone number. With all the fighting and arguing happening at home, something vital seemed to have slipped my mind. Well, dammit. Now you're in trouble. Big trouble, moaned my pathetic little inner voice that never let me off with anything.

Yup, I was supposed to call Destiny sometime that night.

So, you'll have to do it then. Whether you want to or not.

Setting my binders off to the side, I pulled out my phone and sent her a quick text.

Hi Destiny! It's Hunter. You free to talk RN?

Less than ten seconds after clicking send, the screen lit up. A phone call. It was Destiny.

"Hello?" My voice was surprisingly deep, both serenely thoughtful and mature.

"Hunter? Is that you?" a sassy female voice asked.

Smirking, I countered, "I don't know… is this Destiny?"

"Yes, it's certainly me."

She laughed, the sound of her voice unexpectedly soft and

gentle, putting me in a state of relative ease. There came the slightest short lull before Destiny's voice again hummed in my ear. "I was starting to think I wasn't going to hear from you tonight. Especially after what happened at school today... Look, I didn't mean anything by it, Hunter. You know that. Just got a bit caught up. You know, what with Harper poking fun at you and all. That's all it was though, Hunter. A bit of fun, y'know? But anyway..."

She was floundering, stuck for what to say. As for me, well, I was enjoying wallowing in a moody silence. It seemed to be having an effect. Good job we weren't on a video call because she'd have seen that wicked big grin across my face, relishing every painful second.

She sounded awfully guilty for someone who 'didn't mean anything by it'.

But what'd be the point in making an issue of it? As Aunt Jane always said, when the dust settled, don't send a whirlwind roaring through. The dust was still now, at rest, dormant.

"Yeah... well... at least you didn't walk off with my welcome packet again." To this, I couldn't help but smile, a small yawn of exhaustion escaping my lips as well as a chuckle.

There was another awkward pause just before she sighed as if relaxing into the call just a tiny bit, perhaps forgiving herself.

But just when I opened my mouth to say something and break the still pervading silence, Destiny cautiously spoke first. "Mind if I ask you a question, Hunter?"

"Sure. Go for it."

"The lady in the white four-door Porsche who picked you up at school today… was that your mom?"

"No, that's my aunt. I said so, didn't I?" Well, hadn't they asked that at school already, back when one of them made the comment about me setting 'Mommy' on them both?

As I said it, I shifted my eyes toward the unshaded patio window. There was Aunt Jane, sitting alone at the kitchen bar, drinking a glass of red wine and laughing. Not just little chuckles of laughter either, but big whooping breaths of it as if she were watching a Kevin Hart stand-up special or something. Only, I knew she wasn't. It had to be something else entirely.

What's so funny in there? I wondered. Just a few minutes ago, she could barely crack a smile. Now look at her. Wait… is she still on the phone with this Todd Banks? I think she is…

It was Destiny's voice that distracted me from the unsettling thought.

"Oh, I see. Well, your aunt's very pretty. Has great fashion sense too. That's all."

"Thanks, I guess."

That was a weird thing she had said to me. Since when had we had any kind of guardians' admiration club going? And clearly, I wasn't in the mood for small talk, especially about my Aunt Jane. The last thing I wanted to endure was more probing questions about my home life.

Right now, if you want the truth of it, home was an unpleasant place. It didn't fit the supposed meaning of the word. This was not what 'home' was meant to be. It wasn't a welcoming place. Not a safe place. Not somewhere I longed to be each time I was away. Quite the opposite. This was a horrible place. Those two were always going at one another these days.

Especially Aunt Jane, who seemed to think she had to play the big attorney at home as well.

If 'home' were a person, you'd expect someone to say to them, well you should be ashamed of yourself. Home was badly behaved. Home was irksome. It made me feel sick just thinking...

And if this was how the conversation was going to play out, taking us onto the topic of aunts and uncles and moms and dads, I'd prefer it to end sooner rather than later.

"Soooo, Hunter," Destiny began now, a tone of sly intrigue now staining her squeaky-clean voice, "what's up with this rumor going around school? Something about you being some big, important state basketball champ or something? Is any of that true?"

I sighed. "Oh! So, is that what you and Ms. Squirty were trying to harass me about earlier?" Admittedly, I was more than relieved. This whole time, I'd been thinking they were talking about my embarrassing boner moment in the hallway.

In return, Destiny giggled. "Well, duh. What did you think we were talking about?"

"Oh, nothing." I chuckled softly, shaking my head. "Nothing at all."

"So, you are 'Jumper James' then?" Destiny went on, latching onto that newfound thread of intrigue. "The high school basketball phenomenon that everyone's been going on and on about, huh? Well, I'll be—"

"Listen, I'm just a regular guy, okay? Nothing special about me." I didn't want to risk sounding arrogant or coming off as overly cocky, but that didn't seem to stop Destiny from continuing to inflate my ego. "Hey, maybe I can help the team out this year."

"Ha! Help the team." She suddenly laughed in my ear. "Our team sucks the big one. You'll have to literally carry those losers on your shoulders. Either way, you're one of us now."

"One of us?"

"Yeah, silly. You're one of us. A Cloudy."

"A Cloudy?" I didn't know what that meant exactly, but I liked the ring of it. "What's that?"

"You know… Cloud Valley High? Duh. For goodness' sake, Hunter. Are you just putting on an act or are you really this dumb tonight? Get your brain back in gear."

Ha. I kind of liked her this way, loving when she tried to tease and rile me so long as it was all in good humor. And Destiny's voice was now smooth and energetic, a pleasant melody with just a touch of R&B flare. The sound of it made me want to get up and dance right there on the patio, but the feeling quickly vanished as I looked up. There was the scary Aunt Jane staring at me through the window. Aware I'd seen her, she dramatically tapped the face of her wristwatch.

It was the universal sign for, 'Time's up, buddy. Get off the phone and get ready for bed.'

Although not wanting the call to end, I also didn't want my aunt spying on me the whole time. It made me feel like a murder suspect being watched by the cops from the other side of a two-way mirror, except worse. I loved Aunt Jane, but didn't trust her with my true emotions, especially after seeing how mercilessly she'd been cutting poor Uncle Lee down to size.

So, I made sure to contain my raw excitement to just

my voice. Aunt Jane couldn't hear that through the closed windowpane.

"So," Destiny went on. "Tell me a little bit about Illinois then. To quote Harper, 'don't leave out any details… or else…'"

We both laughed at this. Personally, I was more laughing at Harper's ominous threat than Destiny's clever quip. The idea that Harper was always ready to squirt someone with a water bottle she carried around in her purse never failed to make me laugh.

"There's not really much to tell," I answered. "I'm sure you know how it is. Illinois is pretty much a—" At that moment, Uncle Lee slowly opened the patio door and peeked outside at me.

"Is that her?" he whispered, trying to be respectful of my ongoing conversation. When I nodded that it was, a sly smile creased over his tired face. Not wanting to be rude, he quickly gave me a supportive thumbs up and ducked back into the house.

Uncle Lee and I had this unspoken bond, a special closeness and one over which Aunt Jane often secretly seethed. According to Uncle Lee, she considered me the son she'd never had, but I didn't relate to her in the same way. She was not like my mom—not like a mom. But Uncle Lee, well, I could see him as a father figure. Sometimes, I didn't have to say a single word for him to get where I was coming from. He just intuitively knew. I was reminded of this fact, watching him quietly shut the patio door and recede into the house, kind of shrinking to give me space.

I didn't have to tell him about seeking some much-needed alone time.

"Come on, spill the beans, Hunter." Destiny poked and prodded once again. "I'm sure there's plenty about Illinois that you could share. Don't be shy now."

Relenting, I let out a somber sigh. "Honestly, there's not much to say. There's Uncle and Aunt. My uncle travels a lot for his job, so we move around a lot. See? Nothing special."

Destiny, however, kept digging. "What does your uncle do for a living?"

"He's retired from the Navy." Before the words were even out of my mouth, I turned toward the lighted kitchen window. There, illuminated in a standing picture frame of bright yellow light, were Uncle Lee and Aunt Jane. And, surprise, surprise, they were arguing again. Although I couldn't hear what they were saying, it was evident this fight was fierce. My heart plummeted.

Bet she's digging into him again for giving me privacy. If there's anything I know about my Aunt Jane, it's that she hates being told no. Especially when she's trying to get her way. And she loathes me having any kind of private life. It's like she wants me to stay some little boy.

Pulling me back out of my regressive thoughts, Destiny pleasantly chimed in to say, "That's so cool. You've probably seen every state in the whole country by now. Lucky you."

As much as she wanted to chit chat with me about trivial things like geography, it was more interesting to talk about her. Unfortunately, seeing Uncle Lee and Aunt Jane bickering in the kitchen window put me in a kind of sour mood. There was nothing good to say about them now.

So, I quickly shifted the conversation to something else.

Gathering up my scattered school books and binders, I pinched the phone between my shoulder and ear, casually asking, "Why don't you tell me a little bit about yourself, Destiny?"

The line went quiet again as Destiny thoughtfully paused to analyze my open-ended question. She remained introspectively silent as I left the patio and headed back into the house. It wasn't until I was in the confines of my bedroom that she finally cleared her throat to speak.

"What do you wanna know? I'm an open book." Giggling, she added, "Ask and you shall receive, Hunter. No pun intended. But I'm honestly no good at just talking unless you ask me."

"Oh, it's okay then," I said, concerned she was feeling uncomfortable. "Sorry." I hated being asked stuff myself, so the last thing I'd want to do was chase her off by being nosey.

But it wasn't like that, she made clear. "No, really. Ask me. Go on, ask! Please! Ask!"

She wanted the questions. "Okay then," I said. Her enthusiasm was brimming over.

So, choosing my first question wisely, I rubbed my chin and said, "Well… what do you do for fun?" I know, not a great lead-in, but in that time-sensitive moment, it was literally the only thing I could think of to say. Better that than nothing at all.

"Hmm, good question," Destiny teasingly responded. "I guess I enjoy hanging out with my friends. You know, the typical stuff. Social media and whatever. Oh, my parents are pretty cool… when they aren't fighting anyway…"

The last line was what really caught my attention. There it was: a common bond! No wonder we seemed to be drawn together in a strange kind of way. We had fights in common.

Warring parents. Or in my case, a warring aunt and uncle. It would be good to have an ally. I needed her.

Hmm, so Destiny and I aren't so different after all.

"Really? Wow! Then I guess we have that in common. You wouldn't believe the fights…"

"Oh!" she said. She sounded relieved too. "God, I'm sorry to hear that, Hunter."

I sighed now, my voice barely above a whisper, hoping my words were too low to hear, but there was no way to tell for sure as I whispered, "And I really needed someone like you".

Needing to cushion that stupid remark, I shifted gears. "So, do you play any sports?"

"Funny that you ask," Destiny began, that last sad comment of mine now all but forgotten, "I'm the starting point guard for the school's basketball team. Oh, and I'm the first girl in the state of Massachusetts to play on an elite boys' AAU basketball team. So… yeah, there's that."

This was the first time I'd heard Destiny openly brag about herself. Thing was, it didn't come off as smug or cocky at all. Just a matter of fact. I liked that.

I liked that a lot.

Over the next several hours, Destiny and I traded questions and answers, digging deeper into each other's personalities.

And the more I learned about her, the more I felt myself beginning to genuinely like her. It's crazy, but maybe—just maybe—we could be friends. Close friends.

Yes, Hunter was about to make real friends with a girl of all things!

Barely able to contain myself at the idea, my mind swooned. Who would've thought that my first real connection at a new school would be with a girl? How exciting!

I thought of my uncle's face, envisaging him feeling happy for me. Maybe a little bit smug on my behalf, imagining his nephew had snagged himself a girlfriend.

Not that we'd ever become that, Destiny and I.

Just friends. And that'd be more than good enough for me. She was the ally I needed.

But we hadn't even got that far yet. Was the fact of having arguing elders in common really that great a basis for a friendship? And would it be so easy to create one from such a shaky start?

My mind was getting carried away with itself, almost in the same way as Uncle Lee had once forewarned me, "Watch out because some girls—the real needy ones—will be trying out how your surname sounds against their first name before you even know them!"

At that time, I'd howled in laughter as he'd said it, so deadpan. Now, I was nearly as bad!

And just as I felt the conversation reaching its natural climax, Destiny let out a long, sustained yawn. "Wow, it's getting pretty late. Almost midnight already. Time to go, I think."

Checking the time just to make sure she wasn't messing with me, she was right!

It was astonishing to see that it was in fact almost midnight. In less than six hours, we would both have to wake up and get ready for school. How had so much time flown by?

How would I get by on so little rest that night?

That was if I even slept at all. Something had my belly all a-flutter. My new friend.

"Yeah," I eventually answered, wiping my tired eyes with the back of my left hand. "Let's catch up more tomorrow at school."

"Sounds good to me. Good night, Hunter. See you tomorrow…"

"Oh, you bet!" I cringed. That was way too enthusiastic. "I mean, goodnight, Destiny."

Chapter 8

IT WAS BARELY mid-morning when Uncle Lee stormed into my bedroom. Right on schedule, he marched in and began barking his usual script of demands.

"Rise and shine, soldier!" his husky, baritone voice boomed at me, filling the entire room. "No one pays you to stay in bed and sleep the days away!"

You can hardly talk, I thought, reluctant to stir or even crank open an eye. Aunt Jane's always saying how you never stop sleeping. How sleeping seems to be your full time job these days!

Despite how loud he spoke, his tone was singularly clear and grating, like someone squeezing off a small-caliber gunshot in a closed room.

"Time to get up and get to it, son. Come on! Today's the second day of the rest of your life, so you better wipe that grit an' sand outta your eyes and—"

"Yeah, yeah. I know. I know," I murmured from under the mess of crumpled bed sheets stacked on top of me. Still half asleep, a frustrated groan broke free, my hands yanking the comforter farther over my head. "I better get up and seize the day. Carpe diem and all that shit. Blah, blah, blah. Every moment's precious or something. Right?"

"Hunter, no bad language please."

Whoops. Had I really just said that? The s-word? "Sorry. I didn't mean—"

"Yeah, yeah, my ass."

We both laughed at that. There it was again. Our connection. He just 'got' me.

Tentatively, Uncle Lee sighed. The mood of joviality had left us. Shaking his head, he then plunked down on the far edge of my bed. Facing me, he stiffly said, "Not quite, son, not quite every moment's precious. But close. Every moment does count, though. Don't ever forget it."

Pulling the comforter back, I blinked the final vestige of sleep from my eyes and glanced over at him. Did Uncle Lee know how annoying it was to have just caught a glimpse of the clock, seeing I could've stayed in bed a half hour longer? Why get up this early?

But then again, he wouldn't understand that; when he wasn't drinking, which really was only first thing in the mornings, he was up with the dawn, same as when he'd been in the military.

He'd passed that habit on to me. Or let's say he tried hard to pass it on. It would never get any easier for me. I wasn't born a night owl or a lark. Bed called, night or day. That was me.

Riding the surge of tired frustration, I smirkingly added, "Ugh, it's so early. Shouldn't you still be in bed right now? Maybe holding your wife?"

As soon as I said it, my brain sprang into action.

You've stepped a tad too far. It's wrong going for the throat like that, especially since Uncle Lee and Aunt Jane have been fighting pretty much nonstop for days.

But I just couldn't help it. It was a way to retaliate for the early morning human alarm.

These unwanted morning wakeup calls really got on my nerves, a bad start to any day.

Clutching the edges of my blankets with cold fingers, I fell silent, awaiting Uncle Lee's response. To my immense chagrin, he just sat there. Like a man caught in a trance, he unblinkingly stared straight ahead into the shadowy corners of my room.

That was it. This silent mime act continued for several seconds. The staring. The gazing.

I had broken his brain, and the realization of having done it fractured my soul too.

Then, without warning, Uncle Lee snapped out of it, abrupt in standing up from the corner of the bed. Once again, he began to pace back and forth, clearly deep in thought. After almost a full minute of watching him ping-pong across the room, he stopped moving.

Without a word, he turned on his heels and headed out, chuckling to himself. Bizarre.

He'd even left my bedroom door wide open, a very uncharacteristic trait for someone so habitual. I couldn't remember the last time I'd seen Uncle Lee act in such a way, if ever.

When his heavy footsteps gradually faded down the hallway, I tugged the comforter back over my head. From there, the fetal position and sleep somehow reclaimed me.

****

Around 7:00 a.m. or so, my body finally managed to drag itself out of bed and get ready for the day, my first stop the kitchen for a little bit of breakfast before starting another long day of high school. There, sitting in his usual spot at the kitchen table, Uncle Lee quietly ate a bagel with cream cheese. Stepping past for the fridge, I pretended not to notice his hardened glare.

Laughing, I asked, "Morning. How's it hangin', Unc?"

"Hunter," he passively murmured, peering over his glasses at me, thick brow arched.

Again, choosing to ignore his sideways glare, I closed the fridge and sat down at the kitchen table. My hand snatched an orange from the overstocked fruit bowl sitting between us. "Where's Aunt Jane?" A few seconds' pause. I slyly added, "So, did she let you spoon her or what?"

No confusion this time; a major nerve had been struck. As soon as the question left my lips, Uncle Lee stopped chewing, staring down hard at me. If looks could kill, he would have slaughtered me at that kitchen table at least ten times over.

Even sitting a few feet away, I could see the blood pumping at the side of his throat.

Oh boy. Here comes the storm…

Just as Uncle Lee dryly swallowed, his lips pressing tight into an angry white line, Aunt Jane sauntered into the kitchen. Completely ignorant to the tense standoff happening at the kitchen table, she seemed in a fairly good mood, especially for so early in the morning. She was singing Beyonce's hit song 'Run the World'.

With her small, graceful steps, I watched as Aunt Jane danced around the kitchen, bouncing from counter to counter. Like viewing a weird suburban version of a National Geographic documentary, I just sat there and observed the true nature of the common rhythmless white woman in her natural habitat. Oh, and what a sight it was. Did she know just how awkward she looked? Yikes. That's all I can say on that. She continued to sing.

That was when Uncle Lee shifted his stony gaze away from me and over to Aunt Jane.

With a large grin now anchoring his weathered face, he stiffly twisted in his chair to get a better look at her. At that moment, it was unclear what to expect.

But one thing was evident; this situation could've turned really bad, real fast. It would only take one volatile comment or word from either one of them to change the entire mood in the house, good or bad. And if things did go south as they soften did, Uncle Lee and Aunt Jane would be clawing at each other's throats all over again as if intent on making a sport of it.

Another not-so perfect start to a not-so-perfect day.

Suddenly, Uncle Lee stood up from his chair and left the table.

He swiftly approached Aunt Jane as she continued to twirl and sing by the sink. Without a word of warning, he reached out and grabbed her by the thin of her wrist.

My breath caught. How was I—so acutely aware in this moment of being just a boy—meant to react to such a forceful gesture? Was he finally going to snap and hit her? I had no way of knowing for sure. This was heinous, terrible. But the worry was unnecessary, unfounded.

Uncle Lee's demeanor completely changed. Smiling ear to ear, he stepped back and gingerly twirled Aunt Jane around like a ballerina.

Now, they were dancing, and I found myself caught up in a fragment of magic, unexpected and beautiful. Cringeworthy, yes. But so much happier than things had been of late. Any boy would rather cringe and shrink back and writhe on the ground in embarrassment on his elders' behalf than to endure the accusations, the arguments and the misery we had all been through.

It was a joy to behold, and words failed me. They danced as if no one watched.

My eyes seemed affixed to them as they longingly faced each other, eyes sparkling with incandescent light. Their fingers laced together in a corded knot, unable to let go. They kissed, and not just a light peck either, nor was it one of Aunt Jane's infamous air kisses, blown on the wind across a room. This time, their lips locked tight, bodies swooning to the thumping rhythm.

It was the music of their hearts. From where I sat on the other side of the kitchen, their old spark of love was now burning hotter than it had in a long time. Brighter too.

In an instant, they were a happy couple once again. A couple in love, ones who adored and craved and respected each other in a way I'd never believed possible for Aunt and Uncle now.

Even if only for the briefest of moments, that's what they did.

Uncle Lee broke the kiss, aggressively reaching over, caressing Aunt Jane's flat butt cheek.

"Ah, God! That's so gross!" I choked, nearly swallowing a good chunk of orange pulp in the process. "Get a room already! No one wants to see that!" Healthy appetite now thoroughly obliterated, I pushed my chair back, quickly left the kitchen and headed outdoors for the patio.

"Does that answer your question, bud?" Uncle Lee spitefully shouted from the kitchen.

To this, I couldn't help but laugh.

Well played, Unc. Well played…

As the image of them—dancing around like a couple of love-drunk teenagers—gradually faded from the forefront of my brain, it was replaced with something far more unpleasant. The painful memories of my past. Memories I could never escape.

No matter how much I wished for it.

PART TWO

TODD

Chapter 9

ROLLING OUT OF BED, the huge wall clock directly opposite pointed at 8:00 as I grabbed my iPhone from the bedside table. Taking one last glance at sleeping London still curled under the blankets, I tiptoed out of the bedroom into the kitchen, a cup of Peet's coffee calling me.

Opening the lid, I placed my favorite K-Cup pack into the chamber of the new Keurig, waiting for less than a minute before grabbing the twelve-ounce cup of coffee. I headed into the living room to catch up on the latest sports highlights from the night before, my ideal way of starting a beautiful Sunday morning. But the blaring ringtone of my iPhone cut in.

"For God's sake, give it a rest. Who could be calling this early?" The words were breaking through my clenched teeth as a whisper. The caller ID glared at me. It was Blake!

An endless sea of questions flooded my mind, heart racing even faster, still holding the phone securely in my trembling grip. Nearly a year had passed since we'd last spoken or seen one another. What could he possibly want?

On a whim, my thumb hovered over the bright green button for a second as I tried convincing myself against accepting the call, but eventually, I swiped up.

"Blake?" I hesitantly called out, rising from the couch, headed back into the kitchen with the cup of coffee in hand, not even having a purpose in mind. Somehow, awkward calls were always easier to make while walking about. So, walk I did. But I no longer had the desire for a caffeinated pick-me-up, pouring the coffee down the sink, my nerves already sufficiently wired courtesy of Blake who possessed an innate talent of getting under people's skin.

"TB." His voice was louder than I remembered. "How have you been?"

Grabbing the last two Coronas out of the refrigerator, I said, "Enough with the small talk."

The kitchen table was a good spot to perch for a drink.

Drinking a beer this early in the morning was not the best remedy for dealing with the likes of Blake, but I badly needed to take the edge off before something regrettable escaped my lips. A solitary beer could bring instant gratification, taking me away from the stresses of life.

There were plenty of those.

"I need a huge favor," he said casually, the words falling from his lips almost effortlessly. "Can I count on you?"

"Count on me? We haven't even been speaking lately."

My tone sounded irked. Because it was.

I popped a beer top, taking a swig, placing the second bottle down. "It's been over a year, and now you're calling up for favors? You've got some big balls, Blake."

"Listen, TB." The sound of him clearing his throat assaulted the walls of my ears. "I know it's been some time since we last talked or saw one another, but it's taken me that long to forgive you for how you treated Chloe."

There seemed to be no consideration as to how this subject matter greatly affected me. "Leaving her standing at the altar, looking stupid in front of her family and friends, was an unforgivable act. Cutting you off was easier than punching you in the face. You essentially left me with no other choice. Wouldn't you say?"

"Don't remind me." I sighed after a minute of tingling silence, chugging down the beer. "I have been living with the guilt of my cowardice since the day I walked out of that church. I haven't even forgiven myself yet." And why would I forgive myself anyway?

"It's been far too long," he said, not leaving a second in silence, almost whispering. "And you're right, TB! Ghosting you was wrong, but—hopefully like you—I'm a changed man. Touching the hem of Jesus' garment healed me quicker than the bleeding woman."

"Bleeding woman?" The words bounced in my head.

Was he referring to a story from the Bible?

"Okay! Let's say that you have changed and had an encounter with the benevolent Jesus. That doesn't mean you will not have to pay for your wrongdoings another way."

Had I really just called out his wrongdoing without first looking in the mirror?

Talk about the pot calling the kettle black.

"But it does mean I'm forgiven," he intuitively chipped in.

Mentally, I debated whether I had just heard a touch of remorse in his voice, or if this was simply another desperate attempt at getting his way. The last time Blake admitted he was wrong about something was freshman year in college when he'd got caught cheating on his Political Science exam. Maybe, truly, he had changed, and his antics and skirt-chasing days were behind him. I decided to give him the benefit of the doubt, even though my gut was clearly against it.

"The moment I'm able to muster up the courage to face Chloe—and one day, it will happen—will be the moment I ask for forgiveness," I said.

"Today is that day!" he said, pronouncing every word plainly, straightforward and in a monotonous tone, as though talking to a jury of twelve. "Today, you walk in your victory."

"Walk in my victory?" I laughed without humor. "Don't you mean face the lynch-hungry mob at the church?"

Peering over the edge of the patio as I tried to come up with an excuse not to attend church, I heard the loud rumbling of my elderly neighbor's ride-on lawnmower. "Hold on, Blake!" I said, dropping the phone almost immediately, walking onto the patio with the beer still in hand.

"Good morning, neighbor." Mr. Jenkins waved. "Kind of early to be drinking alcohol, don't you think?"

"Mind your business, you old bastard!" I half yelled with my lips closed, raising the bottle in the air, unsealing my lips. "I got one for you, too."

"Not until this ole yard of mine is tamed." He slipped on his goggles and gloves as he hopped back onto his mower. "Have a good day, son."

Walking back into the kitchen, I retrieved the phone from the table, Blake's humming of Amazing Grace welcoming me back to the conversation.

"Blake?" I called out suspiciously, looking down at the phone screen to make sure it was really him on the other end and not someone trying to punk me. As I placed the phone back to my ear, Blake was changing his tune to sing, "…and saved a wretch like meeeeeeeeeeee."

"I sound pretty good, don't I?" He cleared his throat as if ready to sing again. "Your boy is gifted, TB. I'm thinking about joining the church choir."

Was this meant as a joke? It sure as hell wasn't very funny, but unfortunately, he was giving me no say in whatever jokes he decided to tell.

"I'll come to church with you on one condition." As soon as the words were out of my mouth, regret seemed to creep in.

"Anything." He sounded, strangely, beyond relieved. But as yet, he didn't even know what 'the condition' might be. It could still make me escape going to church today.

"You have to agree to go with me. I don't want to face Chloe, her father, or the church alone. You have to promise me this one thing." An uncomfortable silence sat between us, a fulfilled smile curving on my lips. No doubt he was searching for the best words to turn down my request, and then he began singing again.

"Yes, I will lift you high in the lowest valley. Yes, I will bless your name. Yes, I will sing for joy when my heart is heavy, all my days. Oh yes, I will. I choose to praise…" His loud singing caused the smile to fade away from my face.

"Blake? Blake?" My voice, against my will, was raised as I tried jolting him out of his world of righteousness back into reality. "Stop playing around! This is no joking matter."

"Look, you cannot fault a brother for getting caught up in the Spirit. Like the song, 'Yes I Will', I will also be right there by your side, TB. You have nothing to worry about." Though I could not see him, it was as plain as day that his face would be curving in an annoying smile.

"Bet!" I had officially made a pact with the devil, Blake.

There was no going back from this.

"Meet me in front of the church in an hour," he said. The time was 8:45.

"I'll be there at 10:00 on the spot. Won't be earlier than that."

"This is great news, TB. Today is family and friends' day at the church and everyone will be there." The excitement in his voice could even be felt by a deaf man. I cringed under my skin, not seeing the reason for any form of excitement over the issue.

"Everyone?" Suddenly regretting my decision, my mind worked out the faces I shouldn't be seeing, all in one place. "What do you mean, everyone?"

"Everyone who was at the wedding that day." The uncomfortable pit in my stomach coiled into a hot, oily beast of despair, my intuition pulsating with ferocity to call this entire charade off, begging me to realize how bad of an idea going to church with Blake was.

"Now stop making excuses and meet me at church in an hour. Chloe is expecting you."

"Why is Chloe expecting me?" Things were getting worse by the second, and losing control over them was even more infuriating.

"Oh, my bad." Blake's sinister laugh was evidence that I had just walked right into a trap; after all, they didn't call him a devil for nothing. "I thought I told you."

"Told me what?"

No matter how badly my voice wanted to yell, it wasn't going to do me any good in this situation, even as my face turned hot as I chugged down the remaining beer.

"I told Chloe you were coming to church today to explain your side of the story. Oh, and also to apologize. I do hope you don't mind."

As soon as the last word was uttered, the disconnecting sound of the call echoed in my ear.

He truly had hung up the call on me.

Turning around, as I popped the top off the second Corona, London's concerned, sleepy eyes fixed on me from the kitchen door. "Is everything okay?"

"Blake called," I blurted. She meandered to my side, caressing my face with her fingertips.

"Really?" she whispered, using her body as some sort of wall to rest on. "What did he want?"

"He invited me out to church today."

"That's great." Her worried voice suddenly beamed with excitement. "Maybe this is the start of rebuilding your friendship."

"No. He scheduled a meeting for me to meet with Chloe.

I'm not sure if I should go." I sighed, wrapping my arms around her tiny waist as I looked up at her.

"Chloe?" She was emphatic, surprise donning her delicate face. "Chloe, your ex-fiancée?"

"Yeah," I whispered, burying my face in my hands. "Blake thinks I should clear the air with her. What do you think?"

"Listen, baby," her soft voice cooed as she gently lifted my head. "You don't have to do anything you don't want to do, but you have been carrying around this guilt for far too long. Maybe it's time to finally put this behind you. It could be the closure that you both need."

"Yeah, maybe you're right."

The words were barely audible for me, but her comforting smile and warm kisses to my frontal lobe had somehow extinguished the fiery rage alight in me. Once again, I'd allowed Blake to manipulate me, convincing me to betray my conscience, but deep inside, outrunning my past was a bad move. This option, this challenge, had been put before me for a reason.

I had to face this burden head on now. It was the only way to avoid being destroyed by my guilt and I feared not only for myself, but for everyone I loved and cared about.

"Do you want me to come with you?"

Her voice broke through my thoughts as she took my hands

to her lips, kissing them softly, her own way of saying I shouldn't be overthinking the issue.

"That would be great, but…" I pushed myself up from the chair and pulled her into a hug. "…this is something I have to do alone."

Chapter 10

JUST AS PROMISED, I reluctantly pulled into the crowded church parking lot. 10:00 a.m. The lingering feeling of being about to make the second worst mistake of my life tugged at my racing heart, a frustrated sigh sneaking out. How the hell had I let Blake pressure me into attending church to meet up with Chloe? This was insanity itself.

Would she really forgive me for pulling a disappearing act on our wedding day?

I wouldn't have forgiven a person if someone had placed me

in that predicament, and here I was, greedy for her forgiveness. Was I even ready to see her face again?

The look her expression had held when I'd shamelessly told her, in front of the church, that I was in love with another woman flashed through my mind. That face had since been a nightmare I couldn't outgrow. Meeting her today suddenly seemed like a really bad idea.

Turning to my side, my gaze fell on a blue pickup truck parked beside my car, the words Ride or Die inscribed on the driver's side door. Maybe this was the sign I desperately sought. A sign pushing me to make the right decision, which would mean driving my ass out of here before coming face-to-face with Chloe's father, the one person I feared more than anyone.

My hand, stubbornly ignoring the wise counsel of my brain, opened the car door just as my feet joined in, trudging toward the entrance of the church, head down.

My eyes, however, darted around the surroundings, quickly spotting a red Porsche parked next to a car I'd always recognized with just a glance.

That vehicle had been parked up there in the associate pastor's parking spot. It would have been designated for my car had Chloe and I gotten married a year ago.

"Who's that and why's he parked there?" a voice whispered in my ears as I peered closer, trying to get the answers myself. I didn't need to. The driver flashed his high beams and tooted his horn at me, waving like a madman. Of course. The car was Blake's.

"Get in," he shouted, eyes locked in my direction. It confirmed he really was talking to me; an older couple walking into the church had turned to look at him to confirm if he was referring to them. He shook his head no, waving apologetically. They moved on.

As for me, I bee-lined toward the passenger side, sliding into the car.

Not sparing a second to idleness, my eyes were quick to observe the difference in Blake's appearance from the last time I had seen him. He was rocking a full beard these days and was slightly overweight. Though his eyes were obscured behind dark sunglasses, it was evident that despite his physical change, he was the same old Blake.

"TB!" A wide grin sat on his face as he slid his glasses to the tip of his nose, chuckling softly. "I'd have bet my mortgage you wouldn't show up! It's good to see you, old friend."

"I can't say the same…" I wasn't sharing the same excitement, seeing no use in pretending. I reclined my seat and peered out of the front window. "…you were dead wrong for dissing me."

"Yeah, I know." His once excited tone had now turned sober, though his face still forced his lips to curve into a smile as he reached inside his glove compartment, removing a small bottle of clear liquid, which he sprayed inside the car and then at me.

"What the hell is that?" Intuitively covering my mouth and nose, I quickly rolled down the window to avoid inhaling whatever crap that was.

"It's a truth serum!" he blurted, rolling my window up and locking it from his side, the chasms on his face growing wider by the seconds. "Two sprays will drive out any evil spirit."

"Only two, huh? Doesn't sound strong enough." At this point, I couldn't help laughing as I looked at the man beside me, whose face still lit up, probably with the excitement of seeing me again. "Instead of spraying it in the car, maybe you should drink some of it."

I grabbed the bottle out of his hand and pointed it at him. "Open up."

"You are not funny."

His tone had grown serious, his face rid of the grin it once had, as he snatched the bottle from my loose grip, dropping it back into the glove compartment. I had touched a nerve, that much was easy to see when his eyes suddenly bulged out, with large veins popping out on his neck. "You better feel lucky I'm a Christian," he said softly, almost in a whisper.

"Oh, or what?" I laughed a second time, unaffected by the seriousness of his tone.

In all the years I had known Blake, he was all bark and no bite, and his idle threat was just that. There was no reason to believe he had metamorphosed into a killing machine.

"I know it's been a year since we last talked." He dropped his hand on my shoulder and squeezed as he went on, his tone suddenly turning dark. "Look, man... I haven't been completely honest with you. A lot has happened in the past year." He took a deep breath, opened the glove box, and grabbed that bottle of clear liquid yet again. "Maybe we should drink some."

"What are you talking about?" I slouched down in my seat, already expecting the worst, my brain trying to work out the secret Blake must have been keeping from me.

He was rubbing the top of his leg and tapping his foot impatiently, deliberately keeping his face unreadable, gaze remaining so steady.

"What haven't you told me?"

There was some effort to hide the curiosity in my voice, but it was futile. That I noticed.

"Just promise you'll forgive me after I tell you," he said, his voice rid of every emotion, exhaling loudly as he unlocked all of the car doors at once, rolling the windows down, beginning to chant in a language literally foreign to me—unknown and to date, unrecognizable.

Throwing his arms in the air and waving them, he suddenly stopped and smiled at me. "I was praying to God in tongues. Just in case you were wondering."

Oh, hell no! Now I'd seen everything. Blake was possessed!

I reached for the door handle and pulled, trying to get the hell out of there while I still could before whatever was possessing him jumped on me too, pinning me, ripping out my throat.

No chance of escape! The demons could take me now! He'd locked the door again, looking at me sinisterly, as though deliberately trying to get on my nerves. Yet again. Maybe this whole thing was a trap. He had something planned for me! A hit?

My nerves were jangled. For God's sake, abandoning Chloe at the altar hadn't made him want to kill me, had it? That was a stupid notion. Childish. I'd been watching too many thrillers.

"You know me and promises..." I ventured, waiting for his odd confession.

I clenched my right hand into a fist, ready to knock him out if he tried anything, bouncing my knee up and down. Deciding I needed to pray along with him, he grabbed my hand, closed his eyes, and bowed his head, giving me no choice in the matter for at least the second time.

As I mentioned earlier, this man could manipulate me into almost anything. Sitting stock still in a locked car while a possessed man clutched onto my hands with his own sweaty palms before maiming me... Well, somehow, he'd even managed to convince me this was all in my best interests too. Then his voice came. My body relaxed, all in good time too before my rampant jiggling knees dismantled the console and brought it down around us both.

"Father, in the name of Jesus, please forgive me for what I am about to confess to my friend and fraternity brother. I have kept this secret from him too long. You said there is a time to speak and a time to be silent. Well, God, I think it's time to speak and I can only hope and pray that you are standing behind me, steadfastly supporting me in this, my decision, for good or ill..."

Why did he have to bring God into this? God—my own God—should stay out of it!

Closing my eyes, I gritted my teeth in ire as a cluster of thoughts clouded my mind. They were making me squeeze his hand, causing him to slowly open his right eye.

My hand attempted to pull free. He grabbed onto it as if we were engaged.

"What?" he asked, staring at me but refusing to let go of my hands.

"Tell me already!" My patience was paper thin, and he must have heard it in my voice. I heard him sigh, the kind of sigh that said he was also just a tiny bit exasperated with me.

"After I finish praying. I'll tell you then, okay?"

He closed his eyes again, clearly bothered about this 'secret' he wanted to expose. "And try not to interrupt me when I'm praying to our God, okay? I like to get into it… feel the Spirit."

Closing my eyes a second time, I sucked in a deep breath, impatiently hoping the arduous prayer would come to an end, when suddenly, he released my hand.

"Yo, TB!" He smiled broadly and raised his left ring finger excitedly in my view. "Here's what I want to share with you. Your boy finally tied the knot."

"When, and with who?"

Chapter 11

BLAKE BEELINED THROUGH the church sanctuary doors, leaving me standing there scratching my head as the awkwardness of being here—and holding a man's hand—again struck me in the face.

What happened to being here for me? I cursed under my breath at Blake who didn't seem to want to be a part of the meeting between Chloe and me.

A part of me already knew I should never have trusted him to keep his word; he had never been trustworthy before, but the other part of me, to which I had stupidly adhered, told me today could be the day I saw a different side of him. Alas, it had only proved to be the same old Blake!

Standing in the middle of the lobby still patiently awaiting Blake's return, my gaze fell on the one person I had been trying to avoid all morning: Chloe's father. He was standing just a few feet away, talking to a short balding gentleman, dressed in an oversized suit.

Fortunately, his attention was on the man with whom he was having the conversation as I quietly retreated a few steps, avoiding being seen by him or anyone from the ex-wedding party.

I lowered my head, surreptitiously slipping on dark sunglasses in a shallow attempt to blend into the growing crowd. My well calculated attempt at escaping everyone who might recognize me soon became a futile effort. My ever so diligent eyes had already caught a glimpse of Chloe's mother headed in my direction. She had that determined look on her face, the one women get when they set their mind on being the first to snatch a bargain in the Black Friday sale. And she was thundering my way; the wooden floor seemed to vibrate as she darted right for me.

"Where the hell are you, Blake?" The words squeezed through my clenched teeth as I turned, bee-lining toward the men's room, a place where I was sure Chloe's father wouldn't find me.

It was a grievous mistake! Next thing—slam! My ungainly torso collided with the fearsome ogre himself as my left shoulder pummeled into his right pectoral, promptly knocking him off balance. In my moment of disbelief and shock, there was nothing to do but stare in horror.

He began to crumble, staring back with even more surprise, confusion reigning that seemed to say, why isn't this oafish buffoon even offering me any help? He's a waste of space!

The sound of his body hitting the floor, like a jackhammer, echoed in my ears as my heart battered against my ribcage, the world spinning around as though in a slow motion.

I stared down at him with my mouth agape, my impoverished brain seeking to work out the best approach to this problem of mine, but rather too slowly.

Throwing logic to the wind, I skittered past him, darting into the bathroom, taking refuge in one of the stalls. Why I chose to hide is anyone's guess. Wasn't this church visit supposed to be specifically to make peace with Chloe and her family? Well, that was ruined now.

Somehow, it felt more relieving to avoid facing them on my own, and especially not in an embarrassing scenario like this unholy mess in which I'd gotten myself all wrapped up.

It wasn't as though Chloe's father or family were the mafia or something, either. It was just that I'd really have preferred Blake to be around when the whole meeting kicked off.

The last time I'd errantly run into Chloe's father, he'd pulled a gun out on me.

With a cacophony of thoughts running through my head, I looked down. There was a smell.

Oh my God! A floater! Yes, to cap off this excellent experience, there was a plump, pale turd floating in the toilet. Whoever had birthed that humongous log had serious medical problems.

You have gotta be kidding me!

Whatever happened to Christian etiquette? And why are there corn niblets in the poop?

Blake was going to pay. But first, I had to get rid of the offending item or someone would think I'd done it if they saw me leave the cubicle. One embarrassment a day was enough.

I balanced on one foot, pressing my left hand against the stall door for support, using my other foot to flush the toilet because no way on this planet was I going to reach across that… that thing, that giant Zeppelin that lurked in the pan. But that's when things got worse.

The toilet water was starting to overflow, the corn-filled turd making its desperate bid for freedom. Sure enough, it bobbed its way down onto the floor, inches away, gaining ground.

Deciding I had played this game of hide and seek long enough, ready and willing to face whoever was waiting for me on the other side, I ran from the stall.

Right then, two well-dressed guys walked in.

"It wasn't me," I half yelled, storming past the two of them.

"I'm sorry?" one said. My first thought was that he must have been the premium pooper if he was apologizing to me. Then, in the next second, I realized! Oh, he just hadn't heard me.

"Never mind," I said. Before I could exit, the second man skidded and went flying across the room as if on rollerblades, headfirst toward the far tiled wall! He had slipped on something, his leather-soled shoes not doing him a world of favors against a loose poop.

I took that as my cue to depart.

Opening the door to the lobby, I was greeted by the strange emptiness—aside, of course, for the few stragglers standing at the sanctuary entrance.

My brain's logical response was to walk out of church. But since when had my brain been logic-filled in moments of tremendous distress? Instead, I saw myself heading toward the glazed double doors of the inner sanctuary. Looking through them, my gaze fell on two tough looking guys dressed in black suits, standing like statues in front of the congregation.

Well, this was very peculiar indeed.

Their presence, somehow strangely, made me feel safe, as if I no longer had to worry about Chloe's father or some other crazy parishioner attacking me, even if I did deserve it.

Blake, someone I recognized by the back of his head, was seated on the front pew next to Chloe's mother. Soon, the choir walked on stage and began singing 'Situation' by Jonathan McReynolds. It had been ages since I'd last heard the choir, but I was feeling churchy.

Well, I was until a light tap came to my shoulder.

"Are you just going to stand there?" an attractive woman asked, holding the hand of two small kids, catching me off guard.

"My apologies." I pulled the door handle to let her in, but lo and behold, standing on the other side of the door was Sarah, my church stalker.

My heart nearly jumped out of my chest as she stared right back at me, her eyes still holding some form of doubt as to whether or not I was really in front of her.

What was she doing here? And where was Blake's evil spirit repellent when I needed it?

I stepped behind the woman and children in a lame attempt not to be seen.

But it was too late; she had spotted me.

"Welcome to Faith and Love Ministries," she said, greeting the woman and children, escorting the three of them to their seats at the front of the church. As she sauntered back up the aisle, cutting her eyes at me, she stopped in front of an older gentleman with gray hair.

Now, like a signpost, she stood and pointed definitively to the back of the church where I was standing. The old man's head soon turned to follow the direction of Sarah's pointing fingers, as his face became clearer for me to also have a look.

But the face my eyes met was none other than that of old man Chandler. No way!

Chapter 12

MY FEET, UPON seeing Mr. Chandler's approaching figure, took it upon themselves to rescue me from this impending danger. Slowly, they carried me back into the lobby, Mr. Chandler and Sarah forming a barricade in front of me, making it impossible to go forward or sideways. My back was pressed against the wall.

"Well, well, well." Mr. Chandler lowered his head as I turned my face slightly, causing his hot breath to hit my ear. It was a most unpleasant experience, I can tell you.

"I cannot believe you have the gall to bring your evil butt back into the house of the Lord after that little stunt you pulled. You snake. You lily-livered demon. You…"

He'd snapped, my mind dreading what might follow on next as my eyelids seemed to have clamped themselves shut tight, too scared of seeing his tormented, ugly features contorting themselves at me. After waiting for what seemed like hours, but in actual fact were just a few seconds, my eyelids gave way slightly. My gaze met with his eyebrows, which were lowered, appearing closer together than normal. He had an odd vertically wrinkled forehead.

"If I weren't such a Christian… If I were not such a man of God…"

His entire wobbly body quivered and shook like a gigantic plate of Jell-O.

His gaze traveled up to the roof, clasping his hands above his head as I swallowed on my own spittle. "…I would have slapped the evil right out of you, knocking you right into the middle of next year, boy!" He hit the wall beside me with his palm, causing me to jerk in fright as he narrowed his eyes at me even more. As for calling me boy…

Well, it worked. He had transported me all the way back to my school days in one fell swoop. Now, I was that little spotty kid once more, being chastised for not doing my homework again.

Pivoting back and forth between Mr. Chandler and Sarah, I wondered which one of them I would mush first, but before I fell into the devil's trap or landed in jail, I decided to take the high road. They stood there calling me every evil name they deemed fit. Except, of course, Judas.

Finding my voice again, after being baptized by their spittle, I found some good words to say.

"You are right." I smiled, not sure how my declaration would work but feeling just a tiny bit more hopeful. After all, I was not arguing back, was I? I was not standing my ground. Surely, this was giving them what they wanted and would placate them both. Looking from Sarah to Mr. Chandler and finally resting my gaze again on Sarah, I was hoping this time would be different.

"Forgive me for the way I treated Chloe, her family, friends and all the congregants at this fine church. I know I do not deserve for you to forgive me. Nevertheless, I dare to ask it of you."

The words fell softly from my lips as if in the humblest whisper, holding her eyes in mine in a bid to drive my sincerity deeper into her. "I come here today to make peace with all of you, in Jesus' name. I came for no other reason. The Lord knows it to be the truth."

Sarah must have been dumbfounded by my sudden politeness as she stared at Mr. Chandler, her eyes probably asking if he, too, had heard me render an apology just a few seconds ago.

"If Jesus can forgive you, then so can we." Mr. Chandler sighed, taking a step back to give me some room to breathe my own air rather than the shared one I had been made to endure.

I held out my hand toward Mr. Chandler as a peace offering, which he gladly took in his; it was a handshake which ended in him pulling me into an embrace, squeezing me tightly into him. Sarah, who was quick to take the cue, wrapped her arms around my waist, pressing her breasts against my back.

"Whoa!" I freed myself from Sarah the groper, coyly sliding a hand up and down my thigh.

"We are a church of huggers." Mr. Chandler playfully jabbed me in the arm, unaware of the crazy act of Sarah right in front of him. "Isn't that right, Sister Sarah?"

"Yes." Her sinister smile spread like a virus across her lips as she brought her face toward my neck, hot breath caressing my neckline. Had it been someone aside from Sarah, my spine would have tingled in ecstasy, but my body knew better than to allow itself to be affected by her touch.

"Now that Pastor Patterson is off the market—"

Her voice came out as an almost inaudible whisper.

"What do you mean, she is off the market?" the impatient side of me asked, already taking control of things as I grabbed Sarah by both shoulders. I can't pinpoint the exact reasons for my sudden curiosity into the life of Chloe, but somehow, there was a dire need to know.

"Oh!" she looked up at me, seeming to enjoy seeing whatever expression I wore, a soft chuckle escaping her lips in a teasing manner. "So, you don't know?"

"Know what?" I half yelled at her, staring unimpressed, but somehow not getting the response desired. Her reply floored me.

Chapter 13

SO, THIS WAS BLAKE'S deep dark secret? Nah, it couldn't possibly be true, right?

Finding an empty seat at the back of the church, my thoughts wandered back to the earlier conversation with Blake.

Could the woman I'd heard over the background of the phone call have been Chloe?

As I wrestled with these and other unhinged thoughts, the choir slowly exited the stage, a short, portly man dressed in a green shirt and blue jeans taking up position.

Tapping gently on the top of the podium microphone that was securely held in place by the tall stand, he cleared his throat as if he needed to spit out copious amounts of phlegm.

"Testing, testing." Cough, cough, hack...

Ccccrrchhhh, he went. Cough... errrrccch!

He cleared his throat relentlessly, peering into the crowd with a wide warm smile.

"Good morning, church!"

"Good morning!" the congregation shouted back in unison, their faces beaming with smiles, some turning in their seats to get more comfortable.

"My name is Deacon Tracy, and I would like to welcome all first-time visitors. Do we have any first timers here today? If so, please stand so we can be sure to make you feel welcomed!"

My thoughts were blurred as he paced the stage, then I zeroed in on Blake. He had turned in his seat, waving at me, his way of beckoning on me to respond to the first timers' call.

I brushed it off and pretended not to see, but he was adamantly stubborn, refusing to take no for an answer. He got up and nonchalantly headed my way. With a wide smile, he shook hands with everyone within arm's reach as if a politician trying to win votes.

Stopping in front of me, he reduced his height, locking his eyes with mine. A sensation of burning bitter bile was rising inside of my gullet, the weirdest of feelings tugging at my guts.

Does he want me to apologize to Chloe and her family in this manner?

It was sure going to be embarrassing and humiliating to my person, but it was still nothing compared to what I had caused them a year ago. I'd do it if I needed to. Of course, I would.

"What are you doing back here?" He pivoted to the front of the church and pointed. "Come up front. I saved you a seat."

'Well, I wouldn't have known, considering how you ditched me in the lobby the moment we entered the church,' I wanted to say. I just gave him a half smile, nodding as I stood up.

"I have a big surprise for you," he whispered as I felt the urge to call out his so-called surprise right then and there. Instead, I followed behind as he led me to the front of the church.

My eyes were, however, focused on the back of his head as I walked, exercising extreme caution in avoiding anyone whose eyes might catch mine by not looking to my side. I hated myself for having taken off the darkened sunglasses.

Blake pivoted in front of Chloe's parents as soon as we reached the front.

"You remember Todd Banks, right?"

Chloe's father slowly moved to the edge of his seat, staring up at me with clenched fists, wrinkles popping out on his face.

"What is he doing here?"

"Don't worry, Mr. Patterson." Blake came to my rescue, winking at me to calm me down. "I invited him."

"Please forgive me, Mr. and Mrs. Patterson." I glossed over the two of them, the whole church looking on with undivided attention. "I never meant to hurt Chloe or embarrass your family. Blake invited me here today to right my wrongs in front of God, Chloe and you good, God-fearing people, Chloe's loving, wonderful family. Nothing I can say will ever take away the hurt I caused your daughter. I was wrong and shall answer to God for it one day.

"But for now, on this day, I come here to answer to you for my grievous behavior."

I said it all in one breath, unrehearsed too, and though I might say so myself, it was a good little speech. A moment of prime oratory.

My gaze connected only with the cold flagstones of the floor, seeking to spare myself the torture of their intense stares. The unforgiving look on Chloe's mother's face spoke volumes as to everything I needed to know. In other words, she was pissed. To think she had been almost my mother-in-law. Right now, she desired to skin me alive.

Blake, instead of coming to my defense, smiled devilishly at me. It was as though he was watching Jada watch Will Smith smack Chris Rock at the Oscars.

"The only reason I am forgiving you…" Mr. Patterson grabbed me by the back of the arm, pulling me close to himself, "…is because the Bible says I should, but if you ever show your cowardly face in this church again, I promise it will be your funeral."

Squeezing the back of my arm with more force, he stood to his feet, staring deeper into my eyes as his face mottled with anger. He looked like the contents of a can of chopped ham.

Releasing my arm, he ascended the few steps that led to the stage. Carefully removing the microphone from its stand on the podium, he looked down into the crowd with a smile plastered on his features as though he didn't just threaten to take my life a few seconds ago.

"Good morning, saints," he yelled at the top of his voice, smiling widely and excitedly.

"Good morning, Pastor!"

The excited congregation shouted back as I found myself shuffling into a seat beside Blake.

"God is good all the time…!" He stretched the microphone toward the crowd, the smug look refusing to fade from his face.

"… And all the time, God is good!" the congregation shouted, clapping.

"Ohhh, yes! And let me tell you, today is a good day…" His eyes expressed a form of joyful excitement. "…and I have some amazing news to share with all of you." A few people jumped out of their seats, sharing in the senior pastor's contagious excitement.

"But before I share this exciting news, I would like for our special guest to come to the stage and lead us in prayer."

Intuitively knowing who the special guest was, I turned to Blake. "Make sure this prayer is shorter than the one in the car." This service was already taking too long, and I wanted to get this apology over with and get back home to London.

"He is not talking about me, TB."

He blurted this, not sparing me a glance, a defined wrinkle running from the side of his nose to the corners of his mouth as his eyes squinted slightly.

"If not you, then who?" It was a question more to myself than Blake, whose gaze hadn't left Mr. Patterson. Chloe's father flashed a cunning smile at me.

I felt my heart slam against my ribcage, hoping this wasn't what I thought it was.

"Please join me in welcoming Mr. Todd Banks." He clapped slowly, with a few others joining in, reluctantly, before taking their seats.

"What does he mean? I'm gonna open up with a prayer?"

I turned to Blake who now seemed to be deliberately avoiding my eyes, my gaze falling on the menacing look plastered on Mr. Patterson's face. The nasty stare back conveyed this was just the beginning of whatever repercussions he and Blake had planned for me.

"Maybe this is God's way of embarrassing you in front of everyone like you did Chloe." Though his face still held a smile, I could hear the rage flowing through him as he continued to clap. "It's time for you to face your demons, bruh. Time for you to deliver your apology."

The urge to punch him in the face surged through me like a bolt of lightning, though I had to hold myself back in respect to being in the House of Lord. I clenched my sweaty hands in a fist, hoping at any moment to wake up from this nightmare.

Seeing no way out of this mess, I turned to Chloe's mother, who had a mean scowl, her meaty arms folded across her chest, refusing to say a word to me ever since Blake had ushered me to sit with them. She even sat slightly askance as if even pointing the same direction offended her sensibilities. Sweat seemed to be cascading from her pores; she was not pleasantly scented.

"Mr. Patterson is joking, right?" I asked, unclenching my hands, wiping them down at the side of my pants. I don't know why I thought asking her would change things.

My plea for mercy obviously didn't mean anything to either of them.

"Frank is no comedian," she said coldly. "He has never said a funny thing in his life. If I were you…" she whispered, "…I would start praying for a miracle."

I swallowed hard and pivoted in my seat toward the exit that was about fifty yards away. If I took off now, I could make it to the door without anyone tackling me, but then I remembered old man Chandler was sitting at the back of the church with Sarah. The two glorified bouncers seem to be mean mugging me, one of them even cracking his knuckles as if to say, 'You better not think about it'. Was this a Christian church or the Italian mafia?

Taking a deep breath, I jumped to my feet facing the exit, placing one foot in front of the other. Digging my heels into the carpet, I prepared to sprint for the exit like Usain Bolt, but the entire church, as though on cue, stood up and applauded me.

"We forgive you brother Todd!" A voice from the back of the church sprang forward.

"We love you, bro!" another voice shouted.

I found myself gradually getting overwhelmed by this surreal moment.

My feet suddenly became courageous, pivoting from facing the exit and heading toward the stage to meet Mr. Patterson, his features now appearing warmer and friendlier. He widened his arms for a warm embrace, and my feet made their way there. If I hadn't known better, I could have believed I was under the influence of some sort of substance.

This was surreal, incredible.

"I forgive you…" he said with tears in his eyes, hugging me for what felt like a lifetime, "…we all forgive you. Jesus forgives you, so no mortal man must fail to do the same."

"Thank you, sir." I stammered out the phrase as he handed me the microphone, exiting the stage to return to his seat, leaving me baffled by the show of which I had just been made a star.

Lacking ideas on what I was to pray for or how to address the congregation, I closed my eyes and bowed my head, holding the microphone firmly by my side. A deep breath sucked in, to be exhaled softly again before talking privately to God. In that minute, I spoke to Him as if it were just He and I, as if we two were the only ones in the room. It was humbling. It was real.

"God, here I am again, at the same church in which I confessed my faith in your Son, Jesus. I ask that you heal Chloe, her family and all of those shamefully hurt by my cowardice on that fateful day one year ago. I ask that you forgive me and have mercy on me.

"In Jesus' name, Amen."

Clearing my throat, I tapped the top of the microphone to call back the attention of the congregation. Well, dammit. They grew silent immediately, patiently waiting to hear my prayer.

What exactly was it about these people? My mind, not willing to accept that any miracle might have come to pass just yet, tried shaking away the doubt that stubbornly adhered to it.

Clearing my throat for the second time as I closed my eyes, my brain set off engaging in its frenetic efforts to conjure up some sort of a follow-on prayer, as expected. But the only things coming to mind were along the lines of what I had already said. Well, isn't this fun…

"Dear God…" The words reverberated through the microphone. "It was nearly a year ago that I was standing in this very place, addressing the same people who stand before me and you today. I ask that you forgive me for hurting each and every one of them, for being blind to what was right and by allowing myself to be weak in nature. I pray in your Son's name, that your daughter and servant, Chloe, will somehow forgive me for hurting and betraying her."

My emotions were barely in check, betraying me at the time I wanted to be strong the most.

"Take your time son," a male voice called out as I stood motionless for a moment, tears surprisingly tumbling down my cheeks. I tried to continue the prayer, but the words just would not come out. The fury of battle throbbing in my veins, an exceptionally heavy thump came into my heart like an extra powerful beat, making breathing harder by the second.

A gentle hand touched my shoulder, my head involuntarily looking to my side to see who it was, when my eyes met with a face I could never forget. Chloe's.

Wiping away the tears from my eyes with her handkerchief, she slipped her hand in mine. Her smile was sad, sweet, and still shockingly innocent as I stared back with curious eyes.

Why would she smile like this after everything I've done to her?

This seemed impossible, akin to being in a beautiful dream in which someone you have hurt terribly comes to make everything better, behaving as if nothing hurtful ever happened.

The sanctuary was so quiet that you could hear a pin dropping, the congregation probably savoring the entertaining little drama unfolding before their eyes.

I could care less, as all I did was look back at Chloe.

"I forgive you, Todd," she whispered as my heart raced faster, more in relief than doubt.

PART THREE

HUNTER

Chapter 14

MY FIRST OFFICIAL basketball game at Cloud Valley High would take place just before the big fall tournament. We were scheduled to play our rivals, Claire Mountain High, who also happened to be last year's conference champions. Big whoop. I didn't really have any feelings about the classic school-versus-school showoff, only a burning itch to finally set the score straight.

Come game day, the atmosphere in the gymnasium was electrified. Both grandstands were totally packed with anxious fans, each one raving mad with excitement. My teammates and I could all feel that live wire intensity as soon as we stepped foot in the place.

It was the kind of conductive energy you couldn't visibly detect but felt coursing from ceiling to floor. There was no mistaking it. Regardless of the pressure to win, the team and I confidently sauntered our way into the building, looking every bit like a top-notch basketball team.

The best of the best. That was us.

In our minds, we had already won the game.

"You ready, Hunter?" A tough voice suddenly sprang up at my side, pulling me out of the warm depths of my pre-game meditation. To my surprise, Rick now walked in pace with me through the back hallways of the gymnasium; this was the first time he had talked to me directly since tryouts. The working relationship had been tense to say the least.

"I'm ready," I responded, fist bumping him in the process. With an affirming nod, Rick and I joined the rest of the team at the end of a long concrete hallway.

"Okay, team," Coach Dillard said, signaling the team to stop walking and huddle in a circle around him. Under the dim halo of a single uncovered lightbulb, we all stopped and intently listened. "As you all already know," Coach Dillard began, "this is the first game of the season. Against Claire Mountain High, no less. I know everybody is on edge right now. Trust me, I get it. So, I say we go out there and try to have some fun. But, most importantly, let's go out there and win this game! Now, who wants to get a little bit of payback for getting our butts kicked last year? Come on, let's hear it!"

Unanimously, we all jumped up and cheered.

"Here's to an undefeated season!" Rick boisterously added. This brought on another rabble of noise, one much louder and fiercer than the first.

Before the circle could break apart again, Coach Dillard quickly raised his voice to add, "One last thing, guys. I know we already went over the roster for tonight, but there's been a few minor changes. I'm gonna have Rick start the game as point guard. Hunter, you'll start as shooting guard. Everyone get it?"

Rick smiled. "I got this, Coach! You can always count on me!"

Dismissed, we all jogged the rest of the way to the team locker room.

"I thought you were running the point," one of my teammates whispered to me in the hallway. "Wonder why Coach changed it like that. Weird."

My thoughts exactly.

The other kids could tell I wasn't happy about Coach Dillard's last-minute decision to switch me and Rick out. At the time, I thought maybe this was due to me still holding the title of the new guy and was still wet behind the ears.

But that simple explanation didn't sit quite right.

Perhaps Coach thought I couldn't handle leading the team. Not yet anyway. In time, Coach would learn just how wrong he was. Whatever the reason may have been, I brushed off those frustrated feelings and focused my energy on the game.

To better achieve this state of hyper concentration, I quickly changed into my jersey, slipped on my headphones, and tuned out the pre-game chatter of my teammates.

Not even ten minutes later, as we were filing out of the locker room, Coach Dillard pulled me off to the side. He waited until I removed my headphones before he spoke.

"Look, Hunter, I know I originally told you you'd be starting as point guard tonight, but I had to change the call. You're still new here. As head coach, it just wouldn't be wise of me to put you under that much pressure in your first game. Want my advice, kid? You gotta learn to follow before you can lead. Understand what I'm trying to say?"

He paused, waiting for my reaction, but I had none.

Rolling his eyes, Coach Dillard sighed.

"Win or lose, this is my team, Hunter. Not yours. You might've been a big hot shot back in Illinois, but here, I call the shots. My court, my rules. Got it?"

Hot shot from Illinois? I sorely thought. The hell's that

supposed to mean? Where is this clown even coming from with all this?

In that moment, I was determined to show Coach Dillard that he was wrong about me. I was well ready for the challenge. Always was, always had been. As the team huddled up in the hallway for the last time before heading out onto the court, I peered over at Rick, who was standing next to Coach Dillard.

Right away, I could tell Rick was barely keeping it together.

"A-are you s-sure you want m-me to run the point and not Hunter?" he stuttered. Even from a distance, I could see that Rick was sweating profusely, eyes beady and wide with looming fear.

This was a big responsibility, one that could easily hand the game over to Claire Mountain High. Another embarrassing loss of many. Despite what Coach Dillard thought, even Rick knew I was the right choice for point guard. But this concern fell on deaf ears.

"We'll definitely win with you leading the team, Rick. It's a lock," Coach Dillard further insisted, a sly smile pinching at the corners of his beard-stubbled cheeks. "Don't worry about it. Just go out there and give it your best. Same as always, kiddo. No sweat."

That was that; the decision had been made once and for all.

Silently, the team and I jogged the rest of the way. When we finally reached the court, busting through the outer swinging doors of the gymnasium, the stands erupted.

Up on their feet, everyone in the crowd went absolutely bananas for us.

Seriously, I could barely hear my own thoughts over the massive roar that came forth. Riding that wave of audible adrenaline, the team's starting center grabbed a ball from the sidelines, tossed it off the nearest backboard, and slam dunked it.

Again, the crowd went wild.

Moments later, Claire Mountain High came rushing out from the opposite side of the court. They wore flashy red and white warmup jerseys, fully decked out with matching Nike sneakers.

Say what you wanted about them, but their fit was wholly on point. This didn't faze me, though. Not one bit. Really? These are last year's conference champions? These guys? Ha! That's rich. I'm gonna run circles around these chumps. Easy!

I didn't know whether it was the crowd pumping me up or something else entirely, but my confidence was at an all-time high. I didn't just believe we could win the game, I knew we could. I could practically see it in my head. Moreover, I knew I could make it happen.

Looking back over my shoulder to Coach Dillard—who now had one hairy leg hitched up on the team bench as he glanced over the loose pages on his clipboard—I decided it was time to show him what was what. Before the end of this game, he would know exactly what kind of player I was. No doubts. Smiling, I broke from team warmups on the court and approached him.

At first, he only glanced up at me with a concerned look, completely unsure of what I had to say. Once I knew he'd spotted me, I said, "I know you think Rick should run the point tonight and... I just wanted to say... I... I think it was the right decision to make."

Coach Dillard gasped. "You... you do?" He was clearly taken aback by my sudden admission, unsure of whether I was putting him on or not.

"Yeah, I do," I quickly responded. "I mean, like you said, we are playing last year's champions. Pretty big deal, I gotta say. Hey, is it true that they beat Cloud Valley by forty points last time Rick was running the point? Can't remember where I heard that one.

"Hmm... Anyway, if you believe this switch will work in our favor this time, I guess I have no choice but to trust you. You're the coach, right?"

Turning on my heels, I began to walk back onto the court when Coach Dillard dropped his clipboard and frantically called out, "Hunter! Hey! Hold up a second!"

When I pivoted back around and made my way back over to the bench, he whipped the sheen of sweat from his brow, rolled his bloodshot eyes, and windily said, "All right, you've made your point. I take it back. You're gonna start as point guard, not Rick. The way I see it, Claire Mountain High has no idea about you. You're our secret weapon. We have the element of surprise on our side this time. They'll never see you coming. Ha!"

His laugh was sinister, and his pudgy face twisted into a spiteful grimace.

More than anybody, Coach Dillard needed to win this game.

After the brief one-on-one, it was time for both teams to head to their respective benches so the refs could start the game.

Once huddled together, Coach Dillard cleared his throat to make another announcement. "Change of plans, team," he started, glancing over at me with a knowing half-smile. "Forget what I said back in the locker room, boys. Hunter will be starting as point guard. Rick, you're shooting guard. Everyone got it?" Just then, I looked over to see Rick give me an encouraging thumbs up in approval. Rough voice climbing to a blaring crescendo, Coach Dillard raised his hands high above his head and yelled, "Now… let's get out there and win this game!"

Then, the first buzzer rang.

****

With only four seconds remaining in the fourth quarter of the game, the score was tied: 58-58.

And to say the game had been tense up until that point would be a grave understatement.

As last year's conference champion and state runner up, Claire Mountain High had never come close to losing a game against Cloud Valley. Until that night, anyway. This was a close game. Anytime they got the ball, we were right there to stop it. When Claire Mountain High scored a basket, we immediately did the same. Tit for tat. Back and forth the struggle went, all of us pushing our bodies to the physical limit trying to get the upper hand.

Claire Mountain High had found themselves pitted in a serious dog fight.

Jumping up from his corner of the team bench, a very sweaty and intense Coach Dillard wildly signaled to the referee, using our team's final timeout of the game. When the whistle blew, we trudged our way off the court to see what he wanted.

"Listen up, team!" Dillard shouted, hawk eyes darting and nostrils flaring. As he pulled his clipboard out and began badgering us on the next series of plays, I looked over my shoulder to see someone running up and down the courtside.

It was Harper.

I found out earlier that she was the school's yearbook photographer, which explained why she was now crazily snapping pictures of everything. However, it didn't explain why she was also blowing kisses at me. Honestly, I didn't think too much of it at the time. Just Harper being Harper. That was until she charged up the sideline, barged her way into the team huddle and began hugging each of us. One by one.

This included a very blustered and bewildered Coach Dillard.

In all of my years of playing competitive sports, I'd never seen anything like this.

Maybe it was a Cloud Valley tradition I wasn't fully aware of or, more than likely, Harper was just a nutjob. Baffled, I could only stare blankly at her as she pulled her cell phone out of her back pocket and began taking selfies with various teammates, all of this happening right in the middle of Coach Dillard's speech.

"What the hell are you doing, Harper?" I whispered, trying not to draw attention to myself.

"Taking selfies, silly." Without skipping a beat, she moistened her pink lips with her tongue and puckered for the camera. Not a single care in the world.

"HUNTER!" Coach Dillard bellowed, his deep voice carrying well above the rowdy rabble of the crowd. Glaring at me with intense scrutiny, he bared his yellowed teeth at me and growled, "Pay attention! This isn't the time for teenage shenanigans! Stay focused and keep your head in the game! You'll have plenty of time to mingle and flirt at the end of the season."

Leaving the huddle, Harper grabbed one of the team's water bottles from the bench and pointed it at the back of Coach Dillard's head. Spitefully, she took deadly aim.

"How rude…" she said.

Sensing big trouble, I broke from the group and tried to lunge forward. I attempted to grab the bottle from her, but it was already too late. Just as my fingers curled around the plastic bottle, a short stream of the clear liquid squirted out, soaking the back of Coach's shirt.

Ah, great, I thought. I'm done…

A split second later, Coach Dillard spun around and glared

down at me. He then snatched the bottle from my limp hand and brought it to his lips for a big gulp.

"Thanks, Hunter." He belched. "I really needed that."

When the timeout ended, Harper did the unthinkable.

Whirling around, she gave me one hard slap on the butt. The sheer force of the slap made me jump higher than I ever had in my Jordans.

"Bring us home a victory, buns of steel," Harper snickered.

As I rubbed at my sore butt cheek and looked back at her, she took the opportunity to take one last candid photo before scurrying back into the stands.

Once again, she had left me utterly speechless.

But the rest of the team seemed to like it, all bursting out into fits of unhinged laughter. Even Coach Dillard had a sneaky smirk on his face. As I tried to recover from the embarrassing public assault, Coach Dillard quietly summoned me back over to the bench.

Clipboard and black marker in hand, he dropped to one knee, gesturing I should do the same.

"We've all heard about your heroics at Central City Academy," he started, scribbling my name in tight little letters on the finger-smudged clipboard. "We all know you're a state champ. Even so, I think it would be best for Rick to take the last shot."

"Yes, sir." There was nothing else I could say.

In the past, I had single-handedly taken down schools a lot tougher than Claire Mountain High. Way tougher. Of course, Coach Dillard didn't know this, but that didn't matter. I knew Rick wouldn't be taking the last shot. Not if I had anything to do with it, that is. There was no way I was going to pass up an opportunity like that, especially with how hot I was all night.

Time to show everyone who I really was.

Oblivious to my plan, Coach Dillard solemnly nodded.

"I'm glad you understand. Okay, so Rick will inbound the ball to you, setting a high screen on your defender. Your job will be to send the ball up so Rick can sink the winning basket. Then it's game over. Got it? Pass the ball back to Rick for an easy lay-up. That's the plan. Easy does it. Now, go out there and do your best."

When the buzzer sounded, both teams spilled back out onto the court.

Shortly after taking my position, I happened to look over into the stands. There, I spotted Uncle Lee and Aunt Jane sitting together in the crowd. Uncle Lee was enthusiastically cheering me on. Aunt Jane, on the other hand, was too busy fiddling on her phone to even notice me.

Neither one surprised me.

When the referee handed Rick the ball at half court, I turned my attention back to the game.

All the while slapping his clipboard on his upper thigh, Coach Dillard hung on the sidelines and screamed out, "Let's go, guys! Come on! Let's do this!"

As I broke free from my defender, Rick passed me the ball just below the half-court line.

With the clock winding down at my back, I decided it was time to show the rest of Cloud Valley High who the real champs were. Like a bat out of hell, I madly dribbled my way toward the basket, blowing past the other team.

In my peripherals, I spotted Rick anxiously waiting for me to pass the ball.

Not this time.

"Pass the ball, Hunter! Pass it!" Coach Dillard screamed, face redder than a fire engine. Meanwhile, the crowd was going buck wild on both sides of the court. Somehow, I ignored it all, swiftly dribbling past another defender as I pulled up from the three-point line. With mere seconds left on the clock, I took my stance and set the ball sailing toward the basket.

In a matter of seconds, the entire gymnasium fell deathly silent.

It was only when the ball swished into the basket, giving

Cloud Valley High a three-point victory, that the stands erupted with noise. As the final buzzer rang, the fans rushed down from the stands and stormed the court. I did it. We've won the game, and without a second to spare!

Surrounded by hundreds of cheering fans, I spotted Harper running toward me with open arms. Leaping forward, she wrapped her legs around my waist, sending me backwards.

I tumbled to the floor.

"You did it! You won the game!" she squealed. Like everyone else, she was beyond excited. Before I could catch my breath to say something in response, she caught my gaze, puckered her lips, and leaned in close for a passionate kiss.

Taken by surprise, I quickly pushed her off, scrambled to my feet, and began forcing my way through the crowd. I had to find Uncle Lee and Aunt Jane. But before I could, Coach Dillard appeared out of nowhere, grabbing my arm to once again anchor me in place.

With much force, he spun me around. Now, we were facing each other.

"I don't know how they do things over in Peoria," he snarled, hairy top lip quivering with caged anger. "But here, at good ole Cloud Valley High, I make the rules. Do I make myself perfectly clear, Hunter?"

Nodding, I responded, "I hear ya loud and clear, Coach."

I almost laughed but managed to keep my giggles locked up tight.

With a semi-sincere expression, I looked him dead in the eye and added, "Won't happen again. I swear. Next time, I'll be sure to pass the ball."

Softening his grip on my arm, Coach Dillard smiled coyly. "You misunderstand me, son. That's not what I'm trying to say." He took a few seconds to look about the crowded gym, his meaty forearm now slung around my shoulder, before adding, "If you make the shot like you did tonight, then all is forgiven. But if you miss…"

As I stared at him in disbelief, Rick rushed forward to where we stood.

"Helluva shot, Hunter!" he boasted, big goofy smile now plastered across his face.

Like the rest of the team, he was enamored by the swell of positive attention happening all around him. Finally, they had something to be proud of.

"I couldn't have done it without you." Using Rick's intrusion as a way to escape the clutches of Coach Dillard, I made a beeline for the nearest exit. Coincidentally, Uncle Lee and Aunt Jane were there on the other side to meet me. But something was off. They both stood by the exit door, tears streaming down their faces, breath labored and barely able to speak.

"What's wrong, Unc?" I asked. Getting no response, I turned to Aunt Jane.

Finally, Uncle Lee cleared his throat and took a couple deep breaths to steady his nerves. When he finally got himself together, he stood up rigidly straight and saluted me. "Your mom and dad would've been so proud to see you play tonight, Hunter. So proud…"

Needless to say, the thick blanket of silence that followed was tense. I broke down then. In the blink of an eye, I started bawling right there in front of everyone.

"It's okay, Hunter," a familiar soothing voice said from over my shoulder. Wiping the sheen of tears from my face, I looked back to see Destiny. Like two stunning crystals, her eyes sparkled and glistened with fresh tears. She wasted no time stepping in between Aunt Jane and Uncle Lee.

She enveloped me in a great big hug.

Through our combined sobs, I heard something very peculiar.

It was Harper introducing herself to Aunt Jane.

"Hello," she confidently said, one delicate hand stretched forward for a formal handshake. "My name's Harper. I'm Hunter's new girlfriend…"

Chapter 15

I WAS SPRAWLED out on my back in bed, relishing all the mental highlights of that night's glorious victory, when my phone's screen lit up.

To no great surprise, I had received a text message from Destiny.

You up right now? it read. Pls call me. I'm worried about you.

For what felt like minutes, I just held my phone up in the air, all the blood draining from my cold and skinny arms as I stared at that unopened message. That was it.

I had to seriously contemplate whether it was a good idea to call Destiny back or not, especially since she had seen me crying earlier that night. There was never a plan to let any girl to see me in such a state, least of all her. For some reason, she mattered.

For one thing, there was a good possibility that she'd witnessed my public display of intense emotions and had been turned off by it as a sign of fragility and weakness.

As well as that, I was also worried how Destiny might feel about Harper claiming to be my girlfriend. This could be a huge problem for her. In fact, it was a huge problem for me!

Well, hold on, now. Maybe the situation isn't that complicated. Maybe Destiny's just worried about me. Either way, it'd be pretty rude to flat-out ignore her. Might even make things worse…

So, instead of ghosting Destiny, I opened up my phone and found her number. I only got three full rings in before she quickly picked up. "What the hell, Hunter? What happened to calling me after you got home from the game?" Right off the bat, her tone was pissed. I hoped it was just her grave concern showing through. And sure enough… "I was so worried about you."

Taking a deep breath, I paused my answer to glance across the room. There, encased in a tiny glass cube, was my Central City Academy state championship basketball ring.

It sat there on my bedside table, its special protective casing now sparkling with hidden light. Uncle Lee had gone through the trouble of buying it for me, and the outpouring of raw emotion that came with it almost made my head explode. "Eh… I'm good," I finally mumbled back.

It was a matter of trying not to sound too pathetic but melancholy enough. "So… ugh… how're you doing?"

Destiny, unusually quiet this evening, allowed a long, drawn-out pause to pass between us. Finally, after what felt like hours, she softened her tone.

"Hunter…how long have we known each other for?"

Uh oh. That's not good, I thought. Is that supposed to be a trick question or something? Girls always want boys to get the important dates right. Her birthday. The dog's birthday. Her mom's birthday… First time we met. First time we set eyes on each other. First time we swapped numbers. All that garbage! Duh. No idea.

Frantically, I forced my haphazard brain to rewind all the way back to the first day of school. It was some time after Labor Day. So, like a four-year-old attempting to do adding up, I took a few extra seconds to count the months off on my fingers.

Well, if she wants a serious answer, I'll try my best to give her one…

With a great sense of pride, I put the phone back to my lips. "I think we met about four—no—three months ago. Is that right?" I'd made it sound as if I thought it was a test.

But she didn't pick up on it anyway.

This simplistic answer of mine caused Destiny to giggle. "That depends. Did you have to use your fingers to figure that out? Hmm? Be honest."

At this silly truth, we both couldn't help but laugh.

One thing was for sure, Destiny was definitely attentive. Observant to those around her. Although she talked more than most people I knew, I had come to really enjoy listening to her amusing anecdotes. Her voice had a sweet, calming effect to it, like an unavoidably catchy ballad. When we spoke on the phone like this, I'd just close my eyes and imagine she was sitting right there next to me in bed. Together. Talking with Destiny gave me a special kind of inner peace. The kind I so desperately needed in my life.

With an innocent chuckle, she asked, "Can I ask you something? Something personal?"

"Yeah, I guess," I reluctantly answered.

What kind of hell was I setting myself up for? One thing was for certain: a girl like Destiny could never ask just one question. No way. It'd be virtually impossible.

Once the inquisition started, I'd be powerless to stop it. I was now in waiting mode, expecting the floodgates to open and a dozen interrogative personal questions to spill free.

Gulping hard, I tilted my head to the side and thought, For the love of God, please don't ask about Harper. Or why I was crying at the big game. I'm not mentally prepared for that kind of stuff. Not now. Please don't ask about that time I had a big boner in the hallway. Oh God.

Then, it happened. The bombshell question I would do anything not to hear. But was it better than the boner question? Only marginally. They both made me twitch with unease.

"Why do you live with your aunt and uncle? Where are your parents?"

Bolting upright in bed, I had no choice but to blurt out the first thing that came to my mind. A gut reaction. Stumbling all over myself like a buffoon, I drunkenly slurred, "Ugh, h-hold on…I-I have to go get my ice cream out of the oven. Be right back."

Before Destiny could question such a ridiculously stupid statement, my pointy finger had muted the call, tossing the phone on the bed. Then, my feet carried me—dashing—into my bathroom. There, I stared at myself in the mirror, lost in my own indecision.

There had to be some kind of good excuse to end the call.

God, what an idiot…

Talking about my parents was still too hard, and not a place I was ready to revisit. Not mentally or conversationally. Destiny probably wasn't trying to be intrusive or rude for asking, but she was walking a fine line here. One not meant to be crossed.

Why would she want to know about that kind of stuff anyway? Why does she care?

Frustrated and confused, I cranked on the sink and let it run for a few minutes. Just long enough to pull myself back together again.

Not even thirty seconds later, squirting a greasy face wash into my hands and applying it to my cheeks, someone came bursting into my bedroom.

"Hunter?" Aunt Jane's unmistakable voice called out. "Hunter, where are you?"

Why have a door if everyone barges in whenever they please? Ugh, so much for getting some privacy around this place…

As quickly as possible, I rinsed the gunk from my face and grabbed my toothbrush from the sink caddy. In full panic mode, I stuck my head out the bathroom door just in the nick of time.

There she was, Aunt Jane, grabbing up my cell phone from the bed.

"Who's Destiny?" she whispered, staring down distastefully at the screen. She had on that unhappy bulldog face again. My aunt had always been a nosy woman and she wouldn't stop until I gave her something to talk about. Whether I wanted to or not, I had to tell her about Destiny.

Toothbrush still hanging out of my mouth, I darted the rest of the way out of the bathroom. Then, faster than the Flash, I lunged forward and snatched the phone out of her hand, quickly turning away and unmuting the call. She chose not to pursue me. Instead, she crossed the room and stood in the open doorway, scanning my every movement like a hawk.

Regardless, I kept my cool, effortlessly plucking the toothbrush from my mouth.

"Hey, Destiny? Yeah, sorry about that, but my aunt needs me to get off the phone. Could I call you back sometime?"

"Hunter!" Aunt Jane sharply gasped, eyes now slanted at me in scornful suspicion. "I thought Harper was your girlfriend."

Face flushed, I turned back to face her in the doorway. "Harper's not my girlfriend. "Destiny's my—" Luckily, my mouth zipped shut. God forbid.

Likewise, Aunt Jane only continued to glare back from the doorway, arms crossed and brow creased. With one painted fingernail, she insistently tapped the face of her wristwatch.

"Hang up, now. Come on, let's go, Hunter."

"Destiny, I gotta go. The witch has summoned me."

Big mistake.

Even though I should've known better than to bad mouth my aunt in front of Destiny, we both laughed at the cutting remark. Also, it was a great out from a hard conversation. Perfect bail. This call could end without me answering any of Destiny's questions about my parents.

No harm, no foul. Give a little, get a little.

So on and so forth.

"Okay, but make sure you call me back later," Destiny insisted. "This conversation is far from over, buddy."

Geez, give it up already. Did I ask you to be my personal psychologist?

Why are you so pushy about my parents? Who wants to be someone's psychological case study, anyway? An emotional lab rat. No, thanks.

But instead of arguing or complaining about it, I accepted the terms as they were. No doubt this was because there'd been plenty of practice time with Aunt Jane. Nothing was ever negotiable or open for discussion there either. Time to move on.

"Okay." My back turned from the doorway again. "Sounds good. Talk to you soon."

Honestly, that call couldn't end fast enough.

Free once again, I tossed my phone back onto the bed and made a mad dash for the open bathroom. Within seconds, footsteps were thundering up fast behind me. But it was already too late. Dropping my toothbrush in the bathroom sink, I looked up in the mirror. Aunt Jane was hanging over my left shoulder. Eyes ablaze, she scowled at me.

"Please tell me Destiny isn't that black girl who hugged you at the game?"

I had no words.

Chapter 16

'MY LAST' BY BIG SEAN came blaring out of the tiny phone speaker, jolting me awake. This wasn't just any catchy song, however; it was the ringtone set specifically for Destiny.

My arm stretched out and snatched the buzzing phone from my bedside table. It was impossible to stifle a series of yawns. "Hey, Destiny. What's up?"

Though usually over the moon to hear from Destiny, at that late hour, it made me a little peeved. She'd called me well after 11:00 p.m. What the hell, right? Still half asleep, I rubbed my eyes and grudgingly added, "Do you know what time it is?"

"Sorry, can't sleep," she cooed, her voice sounding sort of unsteady. Wobbly. "I've been awfully worried about you, Hunter. Just wanted to make sure you were okay. There's no way I could've slept unless you came on the phone tonight."

Well, I suppose that's nice of her.

"Yeah, I'm good." That was supposed to do it; it was meant to be enough. "So, you can go to sleep now. See you tomorrow."

She heaved a massive sigh. "Hunter, we need to talk."

My eyes were drifting shut though, threatening to set me back to a restful slumber. I was never a night owl or anything like that. Still, I didn't know how to tell Destiny this without also hurting her feelings in the process.

I guess the old saying was true: "There's just no rest for the wicked."

"So," Destiny went on, completely unphased by my evasiveness, "did you get your ice cream out of the oven okay?" Laughing to herself, she then added, "Seriously, nice try, but I know a diversion tactic when I see one."

"Well…can't blame a guy for trying." Words all depleted, I could barely keep my eyes open as I spoke. I was so tired, just wanting to get some sleep.

But before I could even begin to express this to Destiny, a rhythm of heavy footsteps came stomping up to my closed bedroom. Seconds later, the door creaked open.

Uncle Lee, face bland and posture slumped, shuffled in. I could tell right away that he had been drinking. Crouching over my bed, breath hot with liquor fumes, he leaned in close and whispered, "Hey…Hunter…you awake, bud?"

"I am now," I yawned, pretending to have just woken up. This might've worked if he hadn't then noticed the lit phone glued to my right hand.

A sloppy smile unfurled on Uncle Lee's face. Not too subtly, he winked. "Ah, I see. Just wanted to make sure you're doing okay, kiddo. That's all…"

Suddenly, I realized I'd completely forgotten to mute my end of the call. A part of me clung to hope that Destiny wasn't listening, but that would be foolish.

She was far too nosy not to listen.

"Hey, is that the girl that's got your head spinnin' in the clouds? I bet it is," Uncle Lee harshly whispered. Thoroughly sloshed, he spoke more than loud enough for Destiny to hear. Loud and clear. Whatever poison he was drinking had him by the gruff of both horns. Locked in.

To me, it was just another embarrassing moment to add to the day's tally. Yippy-ki-yay.

Before Uncle Lee could further humiliate me, Aunt Jane's silhouette appeared in the open doorway, startling both of us. She had a habit of magically appearing out of nowhere like that, but only at the worst possible moments. That was her special gift. Or one of a few.

"What're you two doing in here so late?" she snapped, instantly suspicious. "What is this, a gentlemen's meeting or what? Am I not invited? Look, Lee, the boy's supposed to be asleep! What do you have, somniphobia? Well if I didn't think so before, you just went and proved it."

To no great surprise, she donned her usual fuzzy pink robe, matching bunny slippers, and a thick, green facial mask. She looked like Shrek. My eyes pinged from one to the other.

Thinking fast, I quickly rolled over on my back to make it look as if sleep had been involved. At the sound of her angry voice, I groaned myself awake, stretching my arms out nice and wide. Thrusting both fists outward, I nearly struck Uncle Lee right in the face, causing him to stumble backward, even adding an exaggerated yawn into the mix. You know, just for good measure.

It had to look real. Hopefully, they would both get the message and leave me alone.

Shambling from my bedside, Uncle Lee looked over his shoulder at the brooding figure still standing in the doorway; you could have cut the air with a knife. It was distinctly chilly between these two. Uncle Lee moodily coughed. Then he thought up a lightning-fast excuse.

Creative too!

"Oh…ugh…I was just praying over the boy. That's all. Christ, Jane, you shouldn't sneak up on people like that. Gonna give me a heart attack. I wanted to send the Lord into him."

"My ass you did!" she hollered. "Tell you what, kneel on that floor again and I'll send the Lord into you with the toe of my slippers in a tender place!"

Ouch.

Flustered, Uncle Lee stormed back out of the bedroom and disappeared somewhere.

As Aunt Jane turned away to watch him go, I took the opportunity to coyly tuck my phone under the blanket, right up against my leg so she couldn't sit on it by accident. Seconds later, she left the lighted space of the open doorway to plop down on the corner of my bed as predicted.

Uh oh, did Aunt Jane see my phone? I desperately thought. Can't tell. If not, then why is she even in my room right now? What could she possibly want to talk to me about?

But then again, if she'd seen my phone, she would've just confiscated it. She was that mean at times like this, especially if she thought Uncle Lee had been involved. But I will never forget how hard my heart was pounding, veins all throbbing under my sweaty skin as I tried to lie perfectly still. Almost a corpse. When I finally opened my eyes all the way, hoping Aunt Jane would be gone, I turned to see her face hovering only inches from mine.

At first, I'll admit, I was a little scared. But now, I was totally creeped out. Horrified. And just when I thought it couldn't get any weirder, Aunt Jane opened her mouth to speak.

"Hunter, why don't you invite your little friend and her family over for dinner this week?"

As she spoke, her green eyes drilled into mine, searching for any inkling of deceitfulness. The way she said little friend was designed to put me down, I was sure.

But there was never any point in retaliation. Never argue with an attorney; this should be a lesson taught to all young people. They will always win, and you can bet your bottom dollar they'll slip in a 'with all due respect' with a snide, superior look before saying something that makes you want the earth to swallow you up and permanently take you away from the planet.

As for inviting my little friend's family too... huh? What was that all about? Weren't families invited to meet other families only when a couple got engaged or something? As far as I knew, I'd made a new buddy at school and that was the size of it. Were we now getting married?

Pulling out another long, far too fake yawn, I rubbed my eyes and dumbly asked, "Huh? What friend? What're you talking about?"

"The girl you're on the phone with. Don't play stupid with me, Hunter. You know, I bet she's still on the call!" She went to rummage out the phone that still lay hidden under the comforter, no doubt wanting to stick it to her reddened ear. Her face must already have been burning up at the sheer imagining of the hot, saucy secrets we were sharing. Only, of course, we weren't. I could swear I heard a click on the line. Destiny must have cut off at the words.

Anyway, Aunt Jane couldn't find the offending article. It languished, almost under my thigh.

God. How embarrassing. Like, 'shrink into your skin and hide' stuff.

Her tone was so stiff, yet also weirdly informal, both angry and charming at the same time. No need to look in her eyes to know that Aunt Jane was now in interrogation mode. And just like a defenseless mouse backed into a corner by a hungry house cat, I had nowhere left to run.

Reluctantly, I sighed, "Yeah… Okay…"

To this, Aunt Jane devilishly smiled. "Good. I look forward to meeting them all."

All? How many family members does she think the girl has? She's a human, not a rabbit.

With that, she stood up from my bedside and left the room, sinister smile still pasted across her green face. She had won her case. No longer could it be a hung jury. I was guilty as charged and she was proudly wearing her victory smile. No doubt she'd wear it for at least three days too.

When the coast was finally clear, I quickly snatched my phone from under the covers, praying Destiny hadn't heard everything.

"I'm back," I whispered, one eye still trained on the empty doorway. To my surprise, she was still there, though I imagined she'd cut the call. Maybe she just hadn't heard anyway, through the thick comforter. "Sorry about that. Privacy is a hard thing to come by around here."

"Welcome back, bright eyes," Destiny cooed, her voice still

cool and collective. "So…what time should the folks and I stop over for dinner tomorrow night?"

Oh my God! No!

A chill ran all the way down my spine. This was way too much excitement for anybody to handle first thing in the morning. Or night. Whatever time it was, I didn't even know. All I wanted to do was sleep now, forgetting all the embarrassing, cringeworthy moments of the last few days. But no, now I had this terrible mess to deal with. This gross mess.

Great. Just freakin' peachy.

So, instead of trying to convince Destiny that a dinner date with my dysfunctional family was a really bad idea, I just decided to cave if it came to it. Anything to end the conversation.

"It's getting kind of late and I'm really tired," I yawned. "Can we talk more tomorrow? Please? We can sort it all out then. Anyway, it was—"

I was about to conjure up some get-out clause when Destiny stepped right in and did it for me! "Haha, don't worry, Hunter! I know she was just teasing you. My aunt's a bit like that too!"

Well, that was a small stroke of luck! At least just for now, I could feign it wasn't true.

At least this way, it was still just slightly possible to pray I'd fall asleep, then wake much later to find my aunt's idea had all been a bad dream, like in the worst self-published novels.

A boy could hope. But my life lately stank, so it was obviously not going to go my way.

Destiny sighed. "Are you sure everything's okay, Hunter? I know you felt upset about—"

She didn't finish. She was going to say, 'when I asked you about your parents'.

Or something like that.

It was always so good talking to Destiny, really. But, at that moment, there was such a lot on my mind, my brain not in the mood for small talk. Especially when it pertained to my parents and the story of why I lived with this ridiculous pair.

However, it would also be impossible to fully suppress the agony of it all alone. Not for much longer anyway. Eventually, I would have to open up to somebody.

It ain't easy being your own therapist, that much was evident.

Again, Destiny gravely asked, "You sure everything's okay? I'm really concerned for you, Hunter, and I am asking genuinely. I hope you know that."

And she was asking genuinely, too. I sensed her probing questions were coming only from a good place, an honorable place full of respect for me.

The tone of her voice was soft, empathic. Sweet and caring.

She was such a nice girl, such a good friend to me already, so lovely, someone it was a privilege to know. A part of me looked forward to sharing. Another part… well, the other part of me, where I held the deep thoughts that had been kept hidden for so long… dreaded it.

There was a dread of the revelation. A dread of coming clean. A dread of being hurt more.

"Yeah, I'm good. It's just been a very long day. That's all."

"Okay then." Destiny sighed, finally giving up on the chase as if she thought I was being awkward or closed off. As if she felt I'd treated her badly.

It cut me. For now though, we would have to let it lie. No way was I opening up now, in the small hours; if we did, I'd never get to school in the morning.

"Okay. Hint taken. Sleep well anyway," she said at last.

"Thanks. You too."

Call ended, I lay back down in bed to go to sleep. Only problem was, I couldn't. My brain just wasn't tired anymore, and there was so much welling anxiety in me. Resigned at the fact that sleep would not come, I rolled myself out of bed and tip-toed into the kitchen for a late-night snack. Lately, I had been what people call comfort eating. Luckily, my body wasn't showing it yet, but it was something to get a grip on before my build turned into a beach ball.

In the darkened kitchen, I grabbed an orange Gatorade and the last two slices of pepperoni pizza from the fridge. After that, I sat at the kitchen table and waited for the oven to preheat. The mystery of why Aunt Jane would want Destiny and her family over for dinner weighed heavily on my mind. But no matter which way I tried to think about it, I could only draw blanks.

There was just no rhyme or reason.

Later, back in the bedroom, there was still time to play Candy Crush on the phone. Maybe then I could get some sleep, though to be honest, it was getting light now, which meant the alarm for school—in the shape of Uncle Lee yelling me out of bed as per normal—was soon to follow. I wasn't brave enough to check the clock. Not now. Just didn't want to know.

But within ten minutes or so, another unwanted visitor appeared at my door. Well, not another as such. The same one. Again. Oh for God's sake, you two! my mind said.

"It's been ten years, son," Uncle Lee softly muttered, somberly making his way into the room. Even though he spoke low, his voice cracked with raw emotion, the tears spilling freely from him. I'd have imagined they'd test to be ninety-nine percent alcohol instead of saltwater as he was still well and truly sozzled and about ready to break down fully. It kind of hung in the air between us and was clear; if he broke down, so would I. Things always went that way.

There was that unknown quantity of a connection between us both, even when I hated him for becoming the drunken bum Aunt Jane accused him of. Even when putting me through hell.

"Can you believe it?" he muttered again, his sad, defeated eyes pushing down to the floor as he approached my bed for the second time in one night. "Ten long years…"

Man, what a sad, sad sight. So abysmal, in fact, that my own eyes were also beginning to brim with tears. I had been unfairly tasked with carrying a burden too heavy for one person to hold. There was also still the question of why God had done this to me. Why choose me to carry this weight around? But it was also down to me to work through. People said so. I knew so.

And yet, even though I knew this, I refused to let it go.

I just couldn't.

Keeping my cool, I flopped my phone to the side of the bed and passively said, "It's been a long day for everybody, Uncle. So let's both try to get some sleep, okay?"

Now standing by the curtained window, Uncle Lee turned away so I wouldn't see him wiping the stream of tears cascading down his jaundiced cheek. But the sobbing was too loud to hide.

A few tense seconds later, he glanced over at me one final time, then slowly walked out of the room. No passing words or acknowledgment. Just as fast and rudely as he'd barged in, he was gone, leaving an empty and darkened void of implacable sadness in his wake.

Chapter 17

THE VERY NEXT MORNING, I woke to find a small, pink envelope resting neatly on my bedside table. Destiny's name was eloquently printed on the front in swooping cursive script. As clear as day.

This was my first major red flag.

Aunt Jane was obviously involved. In my mind's eye, a vision came, one of her sneaking back into my room after I'd fallen asleep for a second time, strategically leaving the envelope by my bed for me to find. Even if it was a trap, there was still a curiosity about what was inside.

Fully succumbing to that inquisitive nature, my still

sleep-laden body rolled out of bed, moving to lock the bedroom door. Only then did I carefully peel open that pink envelope.

Inside was a card.

Ah, I bet this is some kind of fancy dinner invitation, I thought. Clearly one of Aunt Jane's grandiose political strategies. Straight from the company playbook. Think she might've used this one for the upcoming Massachusetts attorney general election too.

I tried to be gentle with the envelope, gently creasing it open for a better look, but accidentally ripping the front at the sound of approaching footsteps. Startled, I quickly put the envelope back on the side table, making sure to place its ripped side facing down. Now, I hurtled to unlock my door. That was a bad idea—to have locked it, I mean. What was I thinking? What would Aunt and Uncle think I was doing if they'd found the door locked? How would I talk my way out of that? God, what a mess! Door duly unlocked again, I dashed to the bathroom.

Shortly, I put on my blue and white Nike tracksuit and matching Air Jordan Retros. But as soon as I stepped foot out of the bathroom, Uncle Lee came storming into my bedroom.

Boy, was he good at scaring the ever-living crap out of me! He was doing it again!

"Oh, what's this?" he asked. I had little time to even realize what Uncle Lee was talking about before he plopped himself down on my bed, ripping open the pink envelope.

Well, so much for being coy and careful about it!

After taking a few moments to read the card, Uncle Lee gazed up, a puzzled look wrinkling his face. "You agreed to a dinner date with Destiny and her family tonight? Here? Really?"

Before I could even respond, he crumpled up the envelope and flung it across the room at me. At the same time, he also slipped the invitation into his pants pocket.

Then, he simply walked back out, chuckling something to himself.

****

"Good morning," Aunt Jane said as I rounded the hallway corner en route to breakfast. My breath must have still been stinking of pepperoni, however. It was only a couple of hours since my so-called midnight feast, which I'd actually indulged in around dawn.

Already, Aunt Jane peered at me intently from over the curved rim of her designer glasses. In between nibbles from her usual morning bowl of tossed fruit, she roughly cleared her throat and added, "Oh, there's a leftover Chick-Fil-A biscuit in the refrigerator if you want it. To push down your pepperoni pizza that I was keeping to take to work today. But never mind."

Talk about giving with one hand and taking with the other! She knew how to score points.

"No, thanks. I'm good." No sense in rocking the boat. Hopefully, any conversation about the pink envelope could be avoided. So, I quickly grabbed an apple from the fruit bowl on the table and sped out of the kitchen, far from Aunt Jane. If I dared stay in there even a moment longer, another uncouth interrogation would be sent my way. It would already be lurking on her tongue.

Too darn early for that mess.

As I headed back down the hallway for my bedroom, phone in hand, Uncle Lee suddenly appeared out of nowhere, rudely interrupting my Instagram browsing.

Like a stereotypical school bully in some corny after school TV special, he forcefully bumped me hard against the wall with his shoulder. What the…?

Aggressively pinning my back against the wall, he leaned in close, whispering, "When're you going to grow some balls and stop letting your aunt push you around like this, huh?" Nose only centimeters away from mine, he bared his teeth. "Be a man, boy! Be a man!"

"You're funny, Uncle Lee," I managed to say, wriggling from his stronghold. "Very funny."

For him of all people to say something like this to me was a classic case of the pot calling the kettle black. What an absolute hypocrite. This guy was practically a hand puppet to my aunt. A tool. And yet, Uncle Lee felt the need to constantly remind me that no one controlled him.

He, and he alone, was the master of his own fate.

It was even stranger because one minute, he'd be all nice to me and be treating me like his best son ever, and the next, he'd switch into mean tyrant mode or just a big school bully. As much as it was horrible to say it or think it, and as much as I wanted to deny this might be the case, it had to be attributed to the wretched alcohol. He drank like a fish. A fish out of water, being exact. It hurt me to admit to myself that on this subject, Aunt Jane was right. I hated the smell of him, and now was left wondering: what if Destiny sees Uncle Lee in this state?

Had Aunt Jane even considered that? Had she factored it in? Maybe she just wanted it to happen so that any prospect of the relationship she believed we were having went right out the window. Maybe Destiny wouldn't even want a friend whose uncle was permanently drunk.

The whole thing made me sad already. Why did my aunt have to interfere like that?

But as the school counselor had once told me, I couldn't live in a world of what ifs.

What ifs were destructive, soul destroying. What ifs prevented us being brave and trying new things in life. So, the planned dinner was going to happen no matter what. I might as well make the best of it. But even so, there was still a nagging doubt. My mind kept taking me back to her comment, that time she'd asked me was Destiny that black girl.

That black girl, that black girl…

Despite the weird Black Lives Matter comment Aunt Jane had made just before my first day of school, I looked forward to getting to know Destiny more outside of studies. It was one of the positive aspects my mind was searching to find. I would make the best of it!

I was excited. Now, I could get to know Destiny outside of late-night phone calls and text messages too, and the odds of this dinner meetup being nothing more than some elaborate PR stunt cooked up by Aunt Jane were reasonably good. 50/50. Not great odds, but worth the risk.

Hopefully, I thought, Aunt Jane isn't fixing to make fried chicken, collard greens and watermelon for dinner.

SECRETS ENEMY

****

I got maybe three feet past the school's front doors before Harper spotted me. It was obvious just by the way she shoved through the crowd that she had been waiting all morning for my arrival.

"Hey, dreamboat!" she exuberantly called out.

She was dressed in ripped blue jeans with a plaid overshirt, a fitted tank top underneath, and her makeup was heavier than usual, to put it nicely. She was looking to impress somebody, and I believed that somebody was me. Engulfing me in a tight hug, she wasted no time lifting her phone up high above our heads for an impromptu selfie together.

Once the ritual was over, she took a step back, giddy.

"Everyone at school is talking about last night's game," she said. "They just can't get over how you led our team to victory. Seriously, that was one of the greatest games in Cloud Valley history. You're officially the second coolest kid at school."

"The second, huh?" I chuckled. "Who's the first then?"

"I am, silly," Harper confidently responded.

Without warning, she snatched my left hand and pulled me closer, pressing her warm body against mine. In the blink of an eye, an unforeseen surge of animalistic lust ran through me.

Like a freight train, there was no stopping it. This was happening. Now.

As I stood there, scared to death that I might suffer from yet another embarrassing hallway boner incident, I glanced over Harper's shoulder. From down the crowded hallway, Rick and Destiny were heading our way. Fast. Just what I didn't need at this, um, juncture.

"I gotta go," I blurted out, pulling myself away from a very clingy Harper. Before she could sink her claws into me again, I slipped into the crowd and hurried off to homeroom.

Never once did I look back.

Mrs. Davis was standing in the open doorway talking with another student when I whisked through to my regular seat. I was safe but for how much longer?

"Great game last night, Hunter," Mrs. Davis said.

From the classroom door, she offered an ecstatic smile.

"Oh…thanks." Everyone seemed to be my fan today. And I honestly didn't care, so tired was I from the lost sleep of the night before.

Exhausted, I set my backpack on my desk, lowered my head, and closed my eyes. Just a little bit of shuteye before things got hectic again. After last night's historic win, I'd be the talk of the town, at least for a little while. This was a celebratory moment—one that would be immortalized in the analogs of Cloud Valley School's history.

Who could blame them for being so excited? Not me.

As the classroom began to fill with students, I soon heard Destiny's voice from out in the hallway, talking loudly with Harper and Mrs. Davis about last night's game.

"There he is!" Harper exclaimed as they all hovered into the classroom together. Again, she didn't hesitate to whip out her phone and start recording me. "Say cheese, superstar!"

Lifting my head from my desk, a small smile twitched at the corner of my lips.

Right on cue, everyone in the room began clapping.

I couldn't stop Harper from snapping selfies of us or from posting them on the school's social media site. Say what you want about her, but she definitely had school spirit.

Too much of it, maybe.

"Ready or not!" she joked, continuing to snap picture after picture. I didn't even get a chance to pose, not that she cared. "Oh, this one is for my private Hunter collection."

"What private collection?" I eyed her suspiciously, hoping that last part was just a bad joke. At times, it was still difficult to work out when she was trying to get a rise out of me and when she was deadly serious. Either way, she ignored me, bouncing back to her assigned seat.

And she laughed the whole way.

But back at her seat, that sickly adulation still didn't end.

"If you really wanna see my private collection, check out my Instagram page for more," Harper casually said, handing me a small slip of paper with her IG handle scribbled on it.

Reaching for my phone, I quickly logged into Instagram to check it out for myself. Sure enough, I was plastered all across her page in an ugly montage of obsession.

Each candid picture was coupled with the hashtag: *#mynewbaehunter.*

This has to be a crime, I thought. *I don't remember ever giving her permission to post all these pictures of me. What the hell? There's gotta be at least fifty on here.*

Maybe more. This is so weird. So creepy... So revolting!

This was not good. I had to find a way to get my face off Harper's Instagram page before the whole school started talking about us. Suddenly, my phone rang, Destiny calling me from across the classroom. "Answer your phone," she mimed, stretching her mouth in all manner of shapes.

Not wanting Harper to eavesdrop on us, like I knew she

would, I got up from my desk and moved to the back of the room to take the call.

"I don't want to put your personal business on blast in front of Harper," Destiny started to say, cupping her mouth as she spoke. "But your aunt sent me a nice long text last night. She was again inviting me and my folks over to your place for dinner. Tonight. Are you cool with that? To be honest, I thought she was kidding, didn't you?"

"Er, yes, I did think that. But it's cool. It'll be nice to get to know you and your folks if she wants to." I put emphasis on the if she wants to. She. Not I.

It took the pressure off me, to the effect that I was going along with it only for my aunt. "She just likes meeting new people. You really don't mind?"

"Oh, no! I don't mind a bit. My mom's like that too. Okay then. That's good."

Then something dawned on me. A horrible realization. Or should I say another horrible realization! "Wait... Um, did you say my aunt sent you a text message? Or did I mishear that bit?" I was appalled. The balls on that lady to go and directly contact Destiny like that!

The cheek, the liberty!

"Yeah," Destiny confirmed. "It was only just after we hung up, like, really late and everything. Got a text from an unknown number, and it only turned out it was your aunt. But unfortunately, like I said to her, my parents are working tonight so they won't be able to make it. But they say they'd love to come another time."

"Oh man, that's a shame," I heard my voice saying. "Never mind. See you tomorrow then."

"No," she said firmly. "You misunderstand! I said I'd come on my own."

A shock traveled down my spine again. So now, only Destiny, 'the black girl', was coming.

Wasn't that going to be a fun evening if my aunt picked on her? I only hoped she would be more gracious and show better manners to Destiny than I'd witnessed from her lately. She surely wouldn't make a young girl feel awkward or unwelcome. I shuddered at the thought.

And there was still the big unanswered question.

"But how…" I just couldn't wrap my mind around how Aunt Jane had even got Destiny's number, and then it dawned on me. Phone records. The Verizon bill. That sneaky witch. She must've been sitting there, going through my phone logs with a fine-toothed comb.

As soon as I realized this fact, Destiny butted in to say, "Well…see you tonight! Can't wait to meet your family! It's gonna be a whole lot of fun!"

Then, she hung up.

As I returned to my seat, Harper was up again. Like a mother showing off pictures of her newborn baby, she garishly paraded around the classroom bragging about her new IG posts.

I, however, was not thrilled. Not at all.

Slumped forward at my desk, I couldn't help but feel incredibly awkward with all the attention bombarding me at school. This only made the dark secret held buried inside for the last ten years that much harder to bear.

A secret far too heavy to carry anymore.

Chapter 18

SPRAWLED ACROSS MY BED, I was busying myself with watching TikTok videos, when Aunt Jane abruptly walked into my room and made herself comfortable beside me.

"What are you watching?" She peered down at my phone screen over the top of her glasses. "I want to see."

"Nothing," I sat up, trying desperately hard to hide the irritation on my face as I looked around the room. Times like this were when I wished I could lock my bedroom door to keep her and Uncle Lee from coming in without knocking. Yes, I had a perfectly good lock on the door. But if I ever locked it, the inquisition that followed from them both made life not worth living.

Attending college out of state after graduation no longer came across as a bad idea, provided it supplied a taste of what privacy really felt like as I hadn't a clue.

"Dinner will be ready at 7:00 sharp," Aunt Jane said.

Deliberately ignoring my cold response, she got up and walked stiffly toward my closet. "Thinking about tonight," she began. "You have to wear the cute outfit I bought you last week."

"What's wrong with what I have on?"

"Sweatpants and a tee shirt are hardly appropriate for dinner, sweetie!" she said softly, opening the closet as she brought out the outfit, laying it across the bed.

"Who's coming to dinner?" I couldn't help the chuckle that fell from my lips, "The President of the United States?"

"If only." She headed back to the closet and grabbed my brown loafers. "Perfect!" She smiled at her work well done.

"I'm not wearing *that*, Aunt Jane."

"But it will look so good on you. And I'm sure your friend will also think so. What is her name again?"

"Destiny." A frown sat on my face as I looked away from her, "Her name is Destiny."

"Yeah, that's right." She began humming an unfamiliar tune. "She is really pretty for a black girl."

"And what's that supposed to mean?"

"Nothing, honey. Just get ready for dinner."

I was sick and tired of Aunt Jane's hang up with the color of a person's skin, and it was time to find out if she truly was a racist.

"Can I ask you a question, Auntie?"

"Anything." She turned her attention to me, taking a seat beside me once again.

Hesitantly, I broached, "Do you have any black friends?"

"What kind of question is that?" She paced the room several times in silence, looking away from me, though her face had already turned red as she rubbed her palms together, scratching the back of her head. "Of course, I have black friends. Doesn't everyone?"

I set my phone down on the bedside table, fully ready for this conversation. "So why haven't you ever invited any of your black friends over for dinner? I'd like to meet them."

Swallowing her laughter, she turned on her heels and walked out of the room, never answering the question. Seconds later, she was back with tears in her eyes.

"You can wear the clothes you have on for dinner tonight.

But please be a sweetheart and put the other clothes back in your closet. The ones I bought you."

"Okay."

Aunt Jane was known for turning the tears on and off like a faucet, and I wasn't sure if these ones were real or not. Either way, I was happy I didn't have to wear that clown suit.

****

"They're here!" Aunt Jane stormed into my room, barking demands at me, ones I had no choice but to meet. I was already in the bathroom adding the final touches to my outfit, needing to make sure I was looking and smelling like a million bucks.

I had decided to wear the shirt and pants Aunt Jane had selected for me after all, instead of the t-shirt attire of earlier, even if Aunt had said the casual look was allowed. Destiny would think I hadn't put in any effort otherwise. A bad idea. I wanted her to be impressed.

"What's taking you so long?" Aunt Jane yelled from the room as I fumbled with my necktie, trying to make the perfect Windsor knot. Heavy footsteps moved closer to the bathroom door.

"I'll be out in a minute." There was a limit to Aunt Jane's patience, and I had crossed it. Before she reached the door,

I stepped out, only to meet with her surprise at seeing me wearing the outfit she had earlier picked out.

A smile of joy and satisfaction lit up her eager face, rendering her speechless.

"You like?" I turned around slowly for her to see the fit from all angles.

"Wow!" The smile on her face grew wider as she looked me up and down. "You look like you belong on the cover of a fashion magazine."

Hugging me briefly, she rubbed the back of my arm gently. "Thank you," she whispered as I looked over her shoulder to see Uncle Lee and Destiny watching us from the door.

"Hey, Destiny." I stared at her like an obsessed fan. It was probably the same kind of look the dreaded Harper kept giving to me—God forbid. But although I wouldn't admit it to myself, I was already crazy for this girl Destiny. And to me, she also looked amazing tonight. Perfect.

She was dressed in a pair of Nike Blazers, a long-sleeve white top and blue jeans that were ripped slightly above her left knee. Her hair was in a ponytail, which fell down to the middle of her back and her makeup was flawless, leaving me awed by her mesmerizing beauty.

Lost in her enchanting looks, I didn't realize quite how long I'd been staring until Uncle Lee grabbed the back of my shirt, tugging at it as he brought me back into reality.

Reaching inside his pants pocket, he handed me a crumpled-up napkin.

Confused, my eyes stared down at it. "Um, thanks but what's this for?"

"To wipe the drool from your mouth. But yes, she's a pretty girl!"

He said it loud enough for all to hear, shaking his head from side to side.

Aunt Jane, on the other hand, glared at me with her hands on her hips, frowning. She wasn't trying to hide it either. She planted her face in her hands.

"What?" I threw my arms in the air as the three of them walked out of my room and headed into the kitchen for dinner, laughing.

"Everyone join hands and bow your heads. Let us pray." Uncle Lee closed his eyes as he began praying for the food. "Thank you for the world so sweet. Thank you for the food we eat. Thank you for the birds that sing. Thank you God, for everything. Amen!"

"Amen!" Aunt Jane's voice echoed through the room. "I love when you pray, honey. Wasn't that the most beautiful prayer you have ever heard? So simple and yet so divine."

She looked at Destiny, then at me.

"Absolutely." Destiny cleared her throat, trying hard not to laugh. "I used to pray that same prayer when I was as young as five. Great job, Mr. Moore."

"Thank you, dear." His voice was deeper than usual. "I only break out that prayer during special occasions. It's an oldie but goodie."

"Oldie or not..." Destiny winked at me and laughed softly. "It's definitely a goodie, and one of my little brother's favorite prayers even now. Maybe Hunter will do Cloud Valley the honors at next week's school rally and pray that same prayer? Though I don't think it will be as cool as your version, Mr. Moore. What do you think?"

"I think it's a great idea, sweetie," Uncle said.

Uncle Lee stood and marched around the table three times before saluting me and Destiny. "And I will be the one seated on the front row cheering the loudest and dressed in my military finest. Now, be a good boy and grab your uncle one of those cold beers from the refrigerator."

I knew my family was trying to make a good impression

on Destiny, but they were so over the top that it made me want to throw up. And I also didn't want Uncle Lee starting on the beers. The back of my neck was bristling in discomfort. This was going to get unpleasant. Soon.

Handing Uncle Lee a Budweiser, I watched Aunt Jane slip on her oven mitts, preparing to remove a glass pan covered with aluminum foil from the oven. I still had no idea what was on the dinner menu, but prayed it wasn't soul food.

"Can I have everyone's attention?" Aunt Jane stood behind Uncle Lee, rubbing down on his shoulders. This couldn't be good. "I want to welcome Destiny into our home and thank her for kidnapping Hunter's welcome pamphlet on the first day of school."

Thanks, Unc! I screamed in my head. I was never telling him a secret again.

"Tonight, I celebrate your and Hunter's friendship. I spent all day in the kitchen preparing this meal that I hope everyone will love. Bon appetit."

Please don't be soul food! I prayed louder in my head, leaning back in the chair, folding my arms across my chest. As though the gods had conspired against me, a tray of undercooked fried chicken, soggy collard greens and burnt macaroni and cheese met with my widened eyes.

Yes, I froze with utter disbelief.

"Destiny..." She handed her the tray. "I hope you like fried chicken, and I hope you don't mind that it's a little pink in the middle."

Why couldn't this be a bad dream? Aunt Jane had never made soul food a day in her life, and now she was pretending to be Betty Crocker. This couldn't be happening. Why me? And besides, wasn't chicken way too dangerous if it was pink in the middle? Should chicken *ever* be pink? Now, I had visions of causing Destiny an outbreak of salmonella and a week off school.

"Thank you, Mrs. Moore" Destiny shot me a look that said, *is this really happening?* as she grabbed a chicken leg from the tray and dropped it on her plate. "It looks tasty. Delicious."

"The mac and cheese is a bit on the dark side, but if you scrape off the charred parts, I'm sure it will taste better than it looks. Plus, it will balance out the chicken legs. One undercooked dish, one over—it all works in the end!" Only it didn't. I wanted to vomit at the thought of half-raw chicken going down Destiny's throat. I worried for whether her guts were already heaving like mine were. As if there was nothing amiss with the meal, Aunt Jane shoveled up a giant scoop of collard greens and mac and cheese, slapping them on Destiny's plate with another chicken leg.

"Oh, and before everyone digs in…" She smiled at the three of us. "…for dessert, I made my grandmother's famous pumpkin pie. But I believe in your culture, Destiny, they call it sweet potato pie." Just then, the doorbell rang.

"I thought you said your parents couldn't make it," I whispered to Destiny.

"They can't," she whispered back.

"Then who's at the door?" I turned to Uncle Lee to get the answers I sought. I knew something was wrong when he mouthed the words 'I'm sorry' and then lowered his head.

"I'll get it." Aunt Jane skipped excitedly out of the kitchen to open the door.

"Hi, Mrs. Moore. I bought dinner rolls."

I knew that voice anywhere. It was Harper!

PART FOUR

TODD

Chapter 19

TRYING TO SNEAK out of the church unnoticed by Blake and Chloe, who were standing in the lobby shaking hands with parishioners, I walked quickly, but very quietly, past them.

I was still trying to wrap my head around the two of them being married. The news of their sudden nuptials had rattled me like a violent earthquake.

Having been emotionally drained by Chloe's father, who had called me out to pray, I no longer possessed the mental capacity to pretend to be happy for either of them. Why would I?

I didn't know why seeing the two of them celebrating together upset me, especially since I was the one who'd left Chloe standing at the altar nearly a year ago. Besides, I had London in my life now, and she was by far the most amazing and beautiful woman I knew.

Still though, seeing the two of them making googly eyes in front of everyone was a really hard pill to swallow.

Coyly slipping through the double doors of the church, my eye caught a glimpse of my church stalker Sarah about fifty feet away, lying comfortably on the hood of my car, with eyes closed, as though she was sunbathing. It was a vision, for sure. A sight for sore eyes.

"Why the hell are you lying on top of my car?" I yelled, sprinting toward her, dreading a situation where her high heels dug into the hood of my brand-new Mercedes Benz.

"You look like you just lost your best friend." Her lips curved in an annoying smile as she slid off the side of the hood. She spread wide her arms as if about to tackle me.

"Come here to Mama. I'll soon have you feeling better." This strange posture was her way of calling me into a hug as a soft chuckle fell from her lips. Either this woman was way crazier than I thought, or someone served her wine instead of grape juice during Communion.

Sidestepping her, I pointed my key at the car to unlock the door, needing to make a quick getaway before the church let out and someone spotted me.

"I'm fine!" I muttered, reaching for the door handle, but pausing when I heard Blake call out behind me. Taking a deep breath, I turned on my heel to face him, but he wasn't alone.

With him now were Chloe, her parents and old man Chandler. Could my day get any worse?

Face-to-face with the religious five, my gaze was fixated on Chloe, who strangely stared right back at me. "You're not leaving so soon?" her voice undulated through the eerie silence, her deep brown eyes narrowing at me like a psychiatrist weighing up the level of insanity in me.

"Yeah." Blake jabbed me in the arm playfully, pulling me from Chloe's enchantment, a smile plastered on his face. "My wife and I would love you to join us for lunch."

"And of course, I would love to join the two of you for lunch," I lied. Seeing the smug look on Blake's face after he'd referred to Chloe as his wife pissed me off even more. A moment longer in his presence and he'd be sure to find his teeth being rammed right down his throat.

"However, my brother and I have plans to watch the Patriots game this afternoon. Maybe another time?" I shrugged, hoping they'd get the message that I wasn't interested in having lunch with them, or anyone for that matter. I was way from being in the mood.

All I wanted was a Black & Mild cigar with a shot of tequila about now.

Sarah, standing behind me, made herself busy rubbing the back of my arm as she watched the whole scene unfold. As the silence dragged and their lingering stares grew increasingly uncomfortable, it was time for me to get out of Crazyville.

Slipping inside my car, I started the engine and rolled the driver's side window down, an act of courtesy so it wouldn't seem I was driving out on them. Which, of course, I was.

"Come on, TB!" Blake's voice broke through the silence as he leaned down and rested his hands on the wound down window. "Don't let my wife down a second time."

That was what you could call a low blow. Devious and manipulative in my view. It was certainly his way of taunting me as he turned around to face Chloe.

"Like I said…" I put the car in drive. "… Maybe another time."

Stepping away from the car, he grabbed Chloe's hand and whispered something in her ear.

I knew her well enough to recognize that her eyes immediately lit up.

"Thank you for agreeing to dinner." Her voice was laced with excitement as a wide grin curved on her face. "We look forward to breaking bread with you. So sweet that you'll come."

"Dinner?" The word bounced back in my head as I stared at the five with a confusion I wasn't even trying to mask. And what did she mean by breaking bread with me? my subconscious whispered. *Is this her version of the Last Supper? It's insane!*

Giving her a half smile, I reluctantly nodded in agreement, staring at Blake with blood pumping angrily in my throat. This was his doing. More fool me for allowing him the pleasure.

"Since you couldn't do lunch because you have plans to watch the game…" Blake's annoying laugh rang in my ears, his eyes sparkling with the devilish thought he had cooked up in his head. "… We'll see you at dinner tonight. I'll text you the address."

Not giving me a chance to change my mind or muster a response, they headed back inside the church with Sarah trailing close behind. It was unchristian, but I was more than relieved that they were gone, reaching inside my glove compartment, grabbing a Black & Mild. Lighting the tip, I inhaled the tobacco to settle my nerves which were reaching an all-time high.

Pulling out of the church's parking lot, my cell phone dinged with a text message from both Chloe and Blake. I parked in an empty spot at the back of the church lot.

Deciding to read Blake's message first, I gave my phone's screen a light tap. His text read:

> You were wrong to sneak out of the church without congratulating me and your ex-fiancée. Didn't think I'd let you off the hook that easily, did you? Dinner starts 7:00 p.m. sharp. Don't be late. And bring that 2012 bottle of Dom Perignon I gave you as a pre-wedding gift before you pulled your disappearing act.
>
> One last thing. Make sure to bring the woman you met on the train. I want Chloe to see exactly who you left her for.
>
> Peace, bruh.

What was it with Blake and his shady behavior? Why was he treating me like the enemy? Whatever happened to being your brother's keeper?

Ever since my fallout with Chloe, he hadn't been the same, the dynamic of our friendship having taken an ugly turn for the worst. Maybe Khalil was right all along.

Perhaps Blake couldn't and shouldn't be trusted.

SECRETS ENEMY

Scrolling back, I clicked on Chloe's text message.

> Todd, Didn't think we'd run into each other again and I haven't completely healed. So many thoughts and questions were in my mind today as you stood at that podium praying through your tears.
>
> I'll never understand why you left me at the altar, looking a fool in front of everyone. But that's neither here nor there. But I do have a question. Why agree to marry me if your heart belonged to someone else? You were wrong, but I've prayed a lot, fasted and sought solace from God, and I forgive you, even if people call me crazy.
>
> Seeing you today made me realize how much I MISS YOU. How could I miss a man who embarrassed me in front of everyone? My mother always told me that the heart loves who the heart loves, right?
>
> I'm gonna stop now before saying something that dishonors my marriage and God. Just know I chose you, not the other way around. You are a special man, Todd Banks, and I wish you the best.
>
> Look forward to seeing you tonight. Ciao!
> P.S. Let's have lunch sometime. My treat!"

A thousand and one thoughts ran through my head, dropping the phone on the passenger seat, driving myself out of the church for good.

Before heading home, I pulled up to the local convenience store to grab a six-pack of Corona and a box of Black & Mild, running low on both and desperately needing to take the edge off.

Exiting the car, I pushed open the heavy glass door. Inside, Mr. Saeed, the store owner, was heavily engaged in religious talk with another customer.

Striding to the back of the store, I grabbed the last six-pack of Corona from the cooler.

Mr. Saeed's eyes lit up on seeing me, his lips breaking into a smile.

Walking from behind the counter, his customary slap landed to the back of my neck. "Where have you been, my friend?"

I rubbed at the back of my neck, irritated. Did he have to do that so hard? "Well, work's been busier than usual." I said, requesting two boxes of Black & Milds to complete my order.

Still bothered by his assault, I angrily dropped the six-pack on the counter.

"Can I ask you a question?"

"Anything." His elbows rested on the counter with his hands clasped in front of him. He looked up at me.

"Why do you always greet me with a slap?"

"It's a friendly American gesture," he said, the beeping sound of the scanner on the items echoing loudly. "It's the gesture they made to me when I first came here, to the community."

Well, that explains it, I thought.

Thrusting my Platinum American Express card into the reader, I ventured, "Perhaps it's time for you to change that gesture before a not-so-friendly person takes offense to it."

"You see…" he began, stuffing the beer and cigars into a crumpled bag that already had a hole in the bottom, pushing it rather roughly toward me. "That is why I hate this country. You want me to speak your language, adopt your customs, but a friendly tap from a law-abiding citizen is offensive. I try to hug you, and you give me a telling off."

"That's not what I meant," I said, raising my palms in a futile attempt at calming a situation that was already getting out of hand.

"Before you go…" He stepped from behind the counter a second time. "… Did you arrest any bad guys today? Isn't that what you do for a living?"

"For the one millionth time…"

The words fell through clenched teeth as I snatched the bag

off of the counter, heading toward the exit. "I am an attorney, not a police officer. I do keep saying…"

"Ah, what's the difference?" He pulled open the door, casting a smile my way, no doubt knowing it was lost on me right then. "They arrest bad guys and you put them in jail, right?"

Giving him a piece of my mind or a lesson in criminal law would have been easy, but instead, I coyly laughed it off, walking through the door. This day had been tough enough without making a situation worse. I had to let things go. So, I encouraged my wandering thoughts.

My mind once again meandered off to thinking about Chloe's text message.

Chapter 20

STRETCHED OUT ON the couch, watching Bridgerton while snacking on a bag of Doritos, was London as I sauntered into the house and bee-lined straight for the kitchen. Normally, I would have greeted her with a hug and kiss, but after today's events at church, I needed a drink way more than I needed a kiss or a hug.

I needed a really strong one at that.

Instead of the usual Corona and lime, I grabbed the bottle of Jose Cuervo tequila and a shot glass from the cabinet above the refrigerator, plopping down at the kitchen table.

"Here's to better days." I lifted the shot glass in midair before pulling it back and gulping its contents down.

Why did something that tasted so good burn so bad?

Quickly filling the shot glass a second time, I swallowed it down with one big gulp, as thoughts of Chloe clouded my mind.

Deciding to reread Chloe's text message, I reached inside my blazer for my cell phone. Perhaps I had misread the message and Chloe missing me was just a figment of my imagination. But no. As I clicked open the message, staring back at me from the screen, in big bold letters, were the words, '**I MISS YOU**.'

How could she claim to miss me after what I had put her through?

Even worse, why was I entertaining the thoughts of having lunch with her when the love of my life was in the other room? I had left Chloe for my new love. Now, I was thinking of meeting her again? That was stupid. In no world would it make any sense. Perhaps I was just another 'typical male' wanting whatever woman was the one he shouldn't or couldn't have.

The thought was abysmal. I hoped to be a better man than that.

Slipping the phone back into my pocket, I got up from the kitchen table, pouring myself a last shot of tequila which I gulped down almost immediately, heading into the living room to confess the whole thing to London; she needed to know.

"Hey, baby!" She muted the TV, peering across the room at me with a smile plastered across her face. "Can you get me something to drink? These Doritos are good, but they sure are dry."

Obliging her request, I turned around, headed back into the kitchen, and grabbed her a Corona out of the refrigerator. Sitting the beer down on the coffee table, I took a seat beside her on the couch. "So, how was church today?" she wanted to know.

Pulling my face closer to hers, she pressed her lips tightly against mine, arresting the reply I thought I had all nicely prepared.

She broke free from the kiss, smacking her lips. "Jose Cuervo, huh? Church was that bad?"

"Yeah." A light laugh fell from my lips as she pushed herself into my arms. "Church was cool, but it was awkward seeing everyone after all this time."

Grabbing the beer from the table as she took a sip, she smiled broadly. "It's never easy to face your past, you know? I'm proud of you!"

I didn't do anything worthy of praise. What could she be proud of?

It wasn't right to tell London about Chloe's feelings after all, just not the right time for a confession, especially after three shots of tequila.

"So how is Blake? Did you talk to the pastor? What did she say? Did you tell her about us?" Her endless questions came at me at once as I began to, against my own wish, feel uneasy about this conversation. Where was Jose Cuervo when I needed him?

Kissing her on the forehead, I said, "We can talk about it later." I got up from the couch and dashed back into the kitchen for yet another numbing shot, my phone's ringtone blaring.

Reaching inside my pocket, a part of me set off screaming in my ears that the caller was Blake, wanting to remind me about the dinner plans. Wrong. Chloe's name danced on the screen.

"What the hell!" I cursed out, almost too loud, a hand over my mouth.

The right thing to do was to ignore the call but curiosity had gotten the best of me; before I knew it, my fingertip was tapping that irresistible green button.

"Hello?" I whispered, sounding a little more nervous than usual. Maybe it was because of the fact that I was already feeling guilty about this call, even before it started.

"Hey, Todd?" Her quiet voice held a mix of anxiety as she took deep breaths in between words. "It's me, Chloe."

I knew that. I could see that, could hear it too. Did she have to be so obvious?

Swallowing hard, her Chloe's voice hitting the depth of my being, that same fingertip pressed mute. I had to think of a way out of the hellish mess I was about to create. London wouldn't take lightly to me talking to my ex-fiancée, the same woman I had left for her.

My ever so efficient brain came to my rescue once again with a well-devised plan that would allow me to have my cake and eat it too.

Unmuting the call, I whispered, "Chloe?" softly.

"Yes, Todd?"

"Can you hold on for a minute?" I muted a second time, without giving her an opportunity to reply to my rhetorical question. Guilt was written all over my face.

London was chugging down the beer as she bounced up and down on the couch like a kid on a trampoline, singing a song to the male lead from Bridgerton.

"Simon, Simon, you so fine, you so fine, you blow my mind. Hey, Simon. Yeah, yeah, hey Simon."

My soft chuckles just might have been louder than I thought.

She immediately stopped her bouncing, looking over at me in the entranceway. A warm smile illuminated her face.

"I don't know what these lovesick women see in Simon Basset, anyway. He's not all that. And I bet his British accent's fake." She pouted, tucking a loose strand of hair behind her ears.

"Mmmmhhhmmmmm!" A genuine laugh escaped my lips as I stared at the beautiful woman on the couch enjoying her movie. My mind suddenly reverted to accomplishing the initial plan. "It's Chloe," I said, waving the phone at her.

"Really?" She leaped off the couch and jumped into my arms, strangely excited by it.

"I love you so much, Mr. Banks."

She kissed me hard, even slipping a little tongue in my mouth. "What does she want?" she whispered against my lips.

Shrugging my shoulders, I voiced, "Don't know."

"Maybe she needs closure…" Her gentle voice was accompanied by her soft hands, rubbing the side of my face. "She deserves at least that."

Turning on her heel, she headed back into the living room singing the Simon song again, as I headed out to the patio, closing the door and taking the phone off mute.

"Hello? Chloe?"

"Am I catching you at a bad time or something, Todd?"

"No!" Annoyingly, my voice was reassuring, as though I really needed this conversation to continue. "I can talk."

I took a deep breath, waiting for her reply or just her voice, but she was silent.

"Is everything okay with you and Blake?" I asked. An awkward silence lingered between us, one that had always been there but this time, felt suffocating.

"Blake is fine, but I'm not." Her voice chose to break through the iciness of the lingering silence. "I have a lot of questions that only you can answer. I know—I should be over it, right?"

"I don't know, Chloe. It's not a question for me, that one. I'm no good at this stuff."

"You seemed good at it to me," she said sadly. "Until you upped and left."

Looking over my shoulder to make sure London wasn't eavesdropping, I headed back indoors just to be sure exactly what she was up to. Curiosity, they say, kills the cat, and my curiosity stopped this call from going to voicemail. Curiosity urged me to pursue it.

Curled up on the couch, falling asleep, was London as I shot her a glance and mouthed, 'I love you'. I pointed to my phone to let her know I was still talking, as she nodded in understanding, allowing me to head back out to the patio, prepared for the worst.

"I'm sorry, Chloe." My head lowered as though she was in front of me. "I never meant to hurt you. I mean, that's trite and ridiculous because since when has leaving someone on their supposed wedding day not been hurtful? But I mean it wasn't planned. Didn't plan to hurt—"

"Well, you did! All right? Do you want me to say, 'oh, it's all right, don't worry about it'? because if you're waiting for that, you'll be waiting a long time, Todd. I do want you to worry about it because it was a disgusting thing that you did to me. A disgusting way to treat me."

Her voice was clogged with tears as she sniffled loudly. "You embarrassed me in front of my family, friends and even God! How could you do such a thing?"

I didn't know what to say or how to respond, but she deserved an answer, even if I hurt her a second time. "I was a coward, Chloe. That's the plain and simple reality. Asking you to marry me when I was in love with another woman was pathetic of me. I was weak and wrong."

"Dead wrong!" she yelled into the phone. "And you will have to answer to God for it."

Why hearing her say I was going to have to answer to God scared me, I didn't know. But it honestly did. "Yeah, I know." I sighed. "Don't think I'm not aware of it."

"But after seeing you at church today…" What? Maybe there was light at the end of this tunnel of mine. "…I realized just how much I really miss you. I sent you a text message after church today. Did you read it? What did you think?"

"Honestly…" I was going to be careful with my words and not try anything that might end up hurting London, "You're married now, so what I think shouldn't matter. I'm happy for you and Blake. Surprised, but happy."

"So you didn't read my text?" Her angry tone was enough to tell me how pissed she was, though I still didn't fully understand why she should be.

"Well, since you didn't have the time to read it, I'll summarize it for you."

"Oh, you don't have to do that. And I did read it." I looked down at my Apple watch, which told me that we had been on the phone for nearly an hour. What had we been talking about?

"Everything changed for me after you left me standing at the altar looking like a fool in front of everyone," she reminded me yet again. "I have been living a lie and I am angry with God for allowing me to meet you. I fell in love with you and thought we would be together forever. Because that's what you'd told me. And then your punk ass pulled a disappearing act. You are not Wesley Snipes."

"What are you talking about?" I got up from the patio chair and headed back into the living room to check on London. By now, she was curled in the fetal position and sound asleep.

"Can you hold on please?" Without waiting for her reply, I muted the call yet again, heading upstairs to pull a spare blanket out of the main linen closet. This was what love was about. Real love. It was about caring for someone, even when they had no idea of the things you did for them as they slept. Carefully draping the blanket over London, I kissed her softly on the forehead.

"I love you," I whispered. She must have heard me, her eyelids opening slowly to find me gazing down on her.

"Hey, you!" She grabbed me around the neck as she pulled me closer. "I love you, too."

"I know, beautiful." I smiled back. "Now get some rest."

"Okay, baby!" She turned on her side and fell right back asleep as I turned off the TV and headed back out to the patio to end the conversation. It was getting out of control.

"I need you to be quiet and listen to everything I have to say, and for the last time, please stop putting me on hold. It's annoying!" she yelled at me as she had never done before. In fact, I had never seen or suspected this side of Chloe; it was scary and at the same time intriguing. Perhaps it held a thread of something faintly alluring. It was appealing when a woman showed feistiness. Slipping back indoors, I grabbed my car keys from the kitchen table and quickly exited the house. The last thing I needed was for London to hear me arguing with my ex.

Safely inside the car, I sent London a quick text message.

> Hey, baby. Headed to the grocery store to
> pick up dinner. Be right back.

Rolling down my window, I slowly backed out of the driveway, forgetting for a moment about Chloe on the phone. "Todd? Are you still there?" she called out, as she should, considering the fact that I hadn't been giving her my full attention.

"I'm still here."

I connected the phone to my car's Bluetooth, turning onto Dorchester Avenue.

"Do I have your undivided attention now?"

"Yes."

"Blake is a good man." I could hear her crying, probably her own heart breaking from her uncontrolled emotions. "He is a very good man, and he's been by my side ever since you turned your back on me. But I can't lie to myself anymore. It's no way to live."

The beep of my phone arrested any reply I might have had for her as I glanced at the caller ID to see it was Blake. What were the odds?

"I'll need for you to hold on again." I clicked over before she could respond.

"TB, my man." His voice was gruff, and I envisaged his face captured in an annoying smirk. "Sorry about throwing you under the bus at church today, but you know your boy is still a work in progress. If God can forgive me, so can you."

"Let me call you right back," I said hurriedly, not interested in his obvious taunting remarks, "I'm on the other line."

"Who are you talking to?"

Gritting my teeth angrily, my fingers dug deeper into the steering wheel, rage flowing through my veins. This was all his fault and right now was the perfect time for him to get a taste of his own medicine. "I'm talking to your wife," I said with a sense of pride. "I'll call you back as soon as I hang up with her."

"Whatever, TB," he laughed without humor, trying hard to mask his own fear. "You are not funny. Besides, I blocked your number from her phone months ago," he said, more to himself.

"Blocking my number from her phone seems kind of childish, don't you think?"

"Not when it comes to brothers like you." His tone was condescending, and that annoyed me more than the words he used.

"What is that supposed to mean?"

"It means brothers like you have a habit of trying to rekindle flames that have already burned out. When the next flame dies, brothers like you pick up the phone to old ones. Besides, you did me a big favor by not marrying Chloe. Your loss, my gain."

"Really?" I pulled up at Stop & Shop, parking in an empty spot near the front of the supermarket.

"Because now she is my wife, so stay the hell away from her before something bad happens to you and that punk twin brother of yours," he threatened in a surprisingly calm voice as the bile rose in my throat.

"Is that a threat?"

"Attorneys like me don't make threats, TB!" His chuckle was as sinister as he was himself. "Let's say it's a promise."

Blake's threat had, however, awakened a darkness inside of me, an uncontrolled darkness that was more frightening than the look on Linda Blair's face in the Exorcist.

And now that it was awake, there was no putting it back to sleep.

The realization of the fact that my twin brother and I had more in common than a shared face was hitting me harder than before; we were one and the same.

"Lose my number, you punk!" I spat out, switching back over to Chloe.

"That must have been one important phone call." Anger was back in her voice, and she wasn't interested in masking it. "What I've been trying to tell you is that Blake's not the man I love, Todd. You are."

The words bounced in my ears as I felt the car spinning me around.

Chapter 21

CHLOE'S CONFESSION caught me off guard, that I must admit, unable to wrap my head around her proclaiming she loved me just weeks after marrying Blake. So had she wed Blake on the rebound from me? It was possible. People did this all the time rather than wind up alone and unloved.

However, Chloe's love declaration was on a sure collision path to destroy my relationship with London and Blake, and I couldn't understand her motivation or gain for sharing this secret.

Unsure of how to disentangle myself from this mess, I placed the call on mute.

This time, I took the action entirely without warning Chloe. This was a call I could do without, one that could bring only confusion, misery, or both. I'd have to muster the courage to end it—the call, the contact, and the rekindling of any kind of connection. It needed doing now.

Reaching inside my glove compartment for a Black and Mild cigar, I returned to the call, staring at Chloe's phone number reflectively. "I never meant to hurt you," I whispered, trying to undo any emotions I must have ignited. "Really, I knew I wasn't the one for you and wanted to make it easier on you by getting out before I caused too much irreparable damage."

"Too late for that," she said plainly, not willing to take back her words. "You should have thought about the amount of pain you were going to bring to my heart before agreeing to marry me. It was outright selfish. You weren't thinking of me at all."

"Look, Chloe, I admit I did wrong. I admit I hurt you. But it's done, it's over, and we're both in other relationships. Can't we move on and just be friends?" I tossed out, hoping that perhaps she might let bygones be bygones. "You're married to Blake, and I'm in love with London."

"Me being married has nothing to do with my love for you, Todd. Oh, and Blake told me about that mysterious girl you met on the train, and how you believe you are in love with her. Is it true that you fell in love with her on the day you met?"

What else had Blake shared with her about me?

"It's true." I didn't know if the pride in my voice was necessary, but I knew London wasn't a mistake. "In one day!"

"Well, Todd Banks…" Her voice was tiny and quiet, unwilling to be swayed by my words. "The same thing happened to me when I met you. So, what are we going to do about it?"

"We?" It was the only comeback I could think of.

"Yes, we."

"Maybe we could pray?" I said slowly, trying not to offend her and at the same time, silence these outrageous thoughts in her head.

"Wow." She laughed. "I would actually love that. However, Blake is calling, so we will have to pick this conversation up another time. See you at dinner tonight."

Another time? Why couldn't the conversation be over now? This was too much for me. Women! It was 5:30 p.m. as I got out of the car and headed inside Stop & Shop. Whizzing through the aisles, I bee-lined toward the wine section and grabbed two bottles of Cabernet.

Dashing toward the long checkout line, I spotted a petite pregnant woman with a shopping cart full of groceries, fumbling through her purse. "It's in here somewhere."

She was muttering, her brown eyes riveted toward me. Time was of the essence, and I had no freedom to wait in this really long queue, my mind conjuring a way to cut the line. "Let me help you out," I offered, walking toward her as I placed the two bottles of wine on the conveyor.

Reaching for the checkout lane divider, I separated items one-by-one. I began to remove her groceries from the cart, neatly placing them on the conveyor behind mine.

"Found it!" She waved the credit card in the air like it was the winning Mega Millions ticket, a relieved sigh escaping her lips.

"That's great!" I smiled comfortingly at her, turning to the cashier, an older white woman, who gave me the death stare. I was wrong for cutting the line, but at the time it seemed like the only right thing to do. Scanning the bottles of wine, she reached out her hand, "ID please!"

Reaching inside my back pocket, it suddenly dawned on me that my wallet was inside my blazer. No ID. Couldn't pay either. I didn't have a dime on me—mortifying.

Face already turning a different shade from embarrassment,

I looked over my shoulder, shifting my gaze from the pregnant woman to the long line of customers behind her.

"Everything, okay?" the pregnant lady asked with concern.

"I left my wallet inside my car," I whispered, feeling like the last crab in the barrel. Talk about instant karma for cutting the line. Turning back to the cashier now tapping impatiently on the bottle of wine, I passed her an apologetic look, the only thing I had to give at the moment.

"Any time today," she said, loud enough for everyone in Stop & Shop to hear.

"It's in my car," I mouthed silently, hoping she somehow had the ability to read lips.

Her loud laugh was like salt added to an open injury as she removed the bottles from the conveyor, voiding my order. "Karma is a biatch."

"It is," I muttered, turning on my heels to exit the store.

"Wait!" the pregnant woman called out as I turned to face her, patiently awaiting whatever ill words she had for me. Only she didn't have any. "I'll pay for them," she offered.

"Today must be your lucky day." The cashier chuckled softly, grabbing the bottles of wine and dropping them back on the conveyor.

"You don't have to do that," I whispered softly as she gave me a reassuring smile. "Today has been a tough day, you know?"

"Whatever you are dealing with"—her eyes followed my gaze—"know that your prayers have been heard. You will find your answers when you put your heart into it."

"I'll be right back." I darted toward the exit to retrieve my wallet from the car, and was out of breath when I returned.

"That will be $379.23," the cashier said to the pregnant woman who was about to slide her credit card in the reader just as I stepped in front of her.

"I got this."

I flashed her a warm smile as I jammed my American Express Card in the reader.

"No!" She waved frantically, her own attempt at stopping me from paying. "It's too much."

"It's my gift to you for being so kind." I grabbed the bottles of wine and extended my arm, "My name is Todd Banks."

"Nice to meet you, Todd Banks." She took my outstretched hand in a handshake before pulling me into a hug that lasted for a few seconds.

"I'm Felicia McCray, and this little one in my tummy is Caleb Ryan."

"What's the hold up?" a male customer from the back of the line shouted. "My wife is going to kill me if I'm not home in twenty minutes."

"If she doesn't hurry up," another angry voice said, female this time, "she's going to deliver that baby in the aisle right here."

It was a fair assessment to say that no one was pleased the pregnant lady and I were taking so long. But somehow, right here seemed as appropriate a place as any to meet one another.

"Before a Malay breaks out in Stop & Shop," I chuckled, handing her my business card, "Call me if you need any legal advice. Have a great day, Felicia and Caleb Ryan."

I smiled, walking out of the store, laughing heartily to myself. My brain reminded me of the cashier calling me a biatch; Snoop Dogg would be proud.

Strapping the seatbelt across my body, I reached for my phone to see there were three messages. One was from Blake, one from Chloe, and the last from Khalil.

Deciding to read Blake's message first, I tapped on his name.

> We need to talk as soon as possible, TB.
> Call when you get this.

Scrolling back, I clicked on Chloe's message:

> Dinner's canceled. Seeing you at church is one thing but having you in my home after my confession is something I can't put London or Blake through. I asked him to call you to cancel dinner. Sorry, Todd, but the heart loves who the heart loves.
> I love you! Ciao!

Taking a deep breath, I scrolled back to have a look at Khalil's message.

> Call me, bruh. It's important!

Pulling out of the grocery store parking lot, I hopped onto Interstate 93.

"Hey, Siri?" I called out.

"What can I help you with?" the female voice responded.

"Call London."

The ring-back tone echoed four times, London's yawns breaking through the silence.

"Where are you?" her sleepy voice asked as she yawned yet again. "I didn't hear you leave?"

"I ran out to the store to pick up wine for dinner tonight," I said as my Apple CarPlay dashboard lit up with a call from Blake. "Blake's calling. I'll call you back. Just hold a minute."

Taking deep breaths as the thoughts of our last interaction

replayed in my head, it was going to take everything in my power not to lash out at him, especially after his threats.

"Relax, Todd," I whispered softly to myself, tapping on his call.

"What's up, Blake?"

"Did you get my text message?" He was humming Amazing Grace. What exactly was with him and that song?

Blake was unaware that Chloe had already warned me about dinner being off. I had to play coy and wait for him to break the news himself.

"Yeah. I got your message. What's up?"

"I was texting to tell you that dinner was off, because my wife wasn't feeling well."

"I'm really sorry to hear that." I tried sounding empathic, but in all truth, I was elated. I no longer had to sit around breaking bread with a fake-ass friend two seconds away from being punched in the mouth for threatening me. "Maybe another day?"

"Dinner is back on!"

"But I thought you said Chloe wasn't feeling well?"

Pulling off the exit as I headed home, driving at a turtle's pace, the thoughts in my mind were centered around, *why me? Why am I always the one caught up in a farce?*

"God is a healer!" he shouted like a Baptist minister on a Sunday morning. "See you at seven." He hung up almost immediately.

Clicking back over to London, I decided to hold off on telling her about Chloe's dirty little secret. It wasn't the time, and dinner at Blake and Chloe's house wasn't the place, either.

What am I going to do now?

Chapter 22

SKIPPING THE DINNER plans with Chloe and Blake was the best option I could think of, not wanting to mount unnecessary pressure on London. Having to share a meal with my ex-fiancée or Blake would be a one-way ticket for Blake to pull, prod and question her about how she and I had met and how effective I was at being a partner. I also had little doubt he'd ask her if she had prepared herself for the day I was bound to walk out on her.

Plus, I talked myself into believing poor Chloe had already been through enough humiliation with me leaving her for London on our wedding day, and I didn't plan to rub more dirt in her face just for Blake's inflated ego. She'd wanted to cancel the dinner, and Blake had somehow got his own way in managing to turn the situation around. It hardly sounded like a great night out.

****

A month soon went by, and life was slowly getting back to usual as I was seated in my office this particular morning, reviewing a final deposition for an upcoming case with the firm's newest attorney, Jane Moore. Jane had recently moved to Massachusetts from Peoria, Illinois, with her husband and sixteen-year-old nephew; this was to be our first case together.

"Good morning, Judy!" I pressed the speaker button, as the landline had rung out a second ago, inviting my green-eyed colleague to listen in.

"Good morning, Mr. Banks," her voice almost whispered. "There is a Pastor Chloe Patterson-Harden here to see you."

What exactly was it with Chloe and showing up uninvited to my office? Was she simply so determined to bulldoze her way into my life, whether I wanted her presence or not?

Getting up from the desk, I headed for the door to find out what Chloe wanted, as Jane grabbed the back of my arm and squeezed it.

"Is everything okay, Todd?" she asked softly, her warm green eyes laced with concern.

"Everything is fine," I said, shifting my gaze from her eyes to the door, inches away from me.

"Do you want to know why I became a lawyer?" She met my gaze and held my eyes, forcing me to focus on nothing else but her. Not that it was exactly a tall order. This woman was striking.

Moving close, she wrapped her arm around me, dropping her other hand on my desk as she secured her body against mine. "I can always tell when someone is lying to me. I have a kid."

Ha, very funny, I thought, throwing her a cynical grin.

Stepping back with her right foot as she sidestepped with her left, she turned the knob to open the door. "Stop by my office to finish reviewing the deposition after your meeting with the pastor." She turned, sauntering out of the office with the deposition file from my desk in her grip.

Popping a few peppermint Altoids to make sure my breath was minty fresh, I took a deep breath and headed toward Judy's cubicle to meet Chloe. Why I cared about my breath, I actually had no idea. I kept telling myself any interest in Chloe had waned. My behavior kept showing otherwise as much as I tried to put a stop to it. "Chloe Patterson!" I greeted her, deliberately maintaining the formality, my face offering a warm but uncomfortable smile.

"Attorney Banks!" A wide grin sat on her face too as she leaped from the couch and darted toward me. "You look great." She chuckled, wrapping her arms around me snuggly.

"So do you."

I held her against my body a second too long, enraptured in her sweet exotic scent.

Chloe was, without a doubt, dressed to the nines. She wore an aqua blue halter dress that gripped her small waist, stopping just a few inches above her knees, and showing off her toned calves and thighs. Her long black hair, styled in a beautiful ponytail, fell down her back.

With an already flushed face, I could hear her quickened breaths as our eyes met.

"I hope you don't mind me stopping by your office unannounced." She smiled up at me, her eyes sparkling as the words fell off her lips. I did mind, very much. Why didn't I say so?

Yet another inconsistency in my behavior of late, ever since Chloe and I had made contact again. "This is not your first rodeo," I laughed. "And I'm sure it will not be your last, either?"

"You know me so well." She giggled, slipping her arm in mine, holding onto it tightly as we ambled the short distance back to my office.

"Make yourself comfortable," I announced, locking the door behind us to avoid interruptions.

Still trying to figure out what Chloe was here for, I pressed the Ctrl + Alt + Delete keys to securely lock my computer, taking my swivel seat behind the desk. "So."

I folded my arms across my chest, peering across the desk at her. "I take it you aren't here in the pursuit of legal advice? Have you come to inquire, yet again, about why I didn't show up to dinner a month ago? Either way, you look delightful. Very pretty."

I meant it. She had injected a lot of effort for me. Why, I still had no idea. I would have thought our respective situations—relationship-wise—made the prospects between us very clear. In other words, there were none. But somehow, she was seeking to impress me. It was flattering.

She never really gave up on giving silent replies either.

This time, though she thanked me for the compliment, she abstained from answering the why question. Why did she come today? She was a master of abstention as she stared through me.

"Whatever happened to us, Todd?" she asked with a voice laced with tears. "I loved you so much. Why did you have to break my heart? You were always saying you loved me."

Swallowing hard on my own spittle, I didn't know the right words to use.

"I don't know." I sighed.

"What do you mean, you don't know?" she asked. "Just be a man and tell the truth."

Getting up from behind the desk, I walked around the room aimlessly. "I don't know what you're looking for, Chloe. I can't give you answers I don't even know myself. But I can make some up if you want me to go that far. You keep asking, and I keep saying I can't answer."

Tell her the truth, a voice yelled in my head. *She deserves at least that. She deserves proper closure, just like London keeps saying. Tell her the truth, and you're respecting London too.*

"Big bad attorney extraordinaire. Todd Banks can successfully defend everyone except himself. You swore an oath to speak the truth before God in a court of law, but you cannot truthfully answer my question. What are you afraid of?" She headed toward me, grabbing my hands as she looked me square in the eyes. "Yes, yes, I know. You already made your choice. The woman from the train, and not me, is the one you love, right?"

"It's a long story," I said glumly, her eyes playing chess with mine.

Standing in the middle of the office holding hands, she pulled me close, pressing her body firmly against mine. Closing her eyes, she reached up as she wrapped her arms around my neck.

"Kiss me, Todd."

All inhibitions had been tossed out of the window as I closed my eyes, bracing my lips for a kiss of a lifetime. London's face, however, flashed in my head as the realization of having almost eaten the forbidden fruit dawned on me. "No!" I pulled, forcefully, away from her, unlocking the office door. "This is wrong on every level. And it's not fair. Not to London and Blake."

My mind was adding, *or to me*. A small part of me felt she was only looking to get her own back for the way I had left her. That she was trying to just break me and London up so I could taste some of the misery she'd had to endure herself after I did the dirty on her not long ago.

After she succeeded in getting London away from me, it was possible she would just return to Blake and they'd both have a great laugh at my expense. No way was that going to happen.

Deciding there was no better time than this to put an end to this unwritten chapter, I was about to tell her the truth she so craved, the truth about my love for London, when a call came.

"Give me a second." I excused myself from Chloe, picking up.

"Sorry to bother you, Mr. Banks." Judy was almost whispering. "You have a call from London Mahone. Line one."

Getting up from my desk a second time, I dashed out of the office, heading for the empty conference room directly across from Jane's office.

"Is everything okay?" Jane asked, poking her head outside her door. I was by now wishing she'd stop asking me was everything okay; it happened seemingly each time our paths crossed. It was going to be worse than having my own mother join me at work if this carried on!

"Family emergency," I tossed back, closing the door behind me. London had never called my office before, and her calling now wasn't something to take lightly.

"Hey?" I answered with urgency. "Are you okay?"

"Yes, baby. Everything is fine." She chuckled, though the tone in her voice told me she wasn't being completely honest.

"Okay," I kicked my feet up on the conference table, as I took a seat. "So, what's up?"

"I hope you're sitting down." Her voice was filled with a childlike excitement.

"I am." My fingers were already trembling with fear.

Please do not tell me you are pregnant, I begged in my head. We had always been extra careful and protected ourselves for times like this, but still one could never be too careful.

Please don't be pregnant. Please don't be pregnant. Damn, Jose Cuervo, I cursed through sealed lips, as beads of sweat formed on my forehead.

"I just landed my dream commission!" she screamed, her voice beaming with excitement.

"What did you say?" Nearly hyperventilating, I moved to the edge of the chair and clutched the back of my head, relieved.

"I was just offered the project of my dreams," she said a second time, reaffirming that I had heard correctly the first time.

"That's great news, London." I was relieved beyond belief and nearly in tears, more because she wasn't pregnant after all. "Tell me more!"

"The advertising company I told you about a few weeks ago contacted me today. They want to purchase and display my artwork in their corporate office. They are also going to pay me big bucks to paint a new series of pieces for the office."

"This is great news, baby." I got up from the desk and

walked out of the conference room to share the good news with Judy, who was visibly absent. Looking down the short hall, I spotted her standing in the doorway of Jane's office. Worse still, they were both with Chloe.

What could they be talking about?

Back in the conference room, I closed the door behind me. "So, when do you start?"

"That's the thing." Her voice was suddenly melancholic. "The corporate office has moved from Boston to a town in Illinois called Peoria. I'm flying out tonight."

"What do you mean, you're flying out tonight?" Was this the universe's way of punishing me? At least she wouldn't have had to fly out if it had been pregnancy news.

"How long will you be gone?"

"No more than four months," she mouthed softly, obviously sensing my own sadness. "That's how long it will take for me to complete the assignment. I'm so sorry, baby. But I knew you'd understand. You've always been my biggest fan."

Now she'd said that, she had me cornered in a position in which I couldn't complain.

"Why can't you paint the pictures here and send them across?" I asked, my brain working around the clock in conjuring up another way for her to have her dream job and still be with me.

"If they were hanging paintings, yes…" She sighed. "But these are murals."

Crap!

Who was I to stand in the way of her dreams? But I had to be honest with my feelings; four months seemed like such a long time, especially after it had taken me over a year to find her. Why did it suddenly feel as if she was slipping out of my grasp, again?

"Painting's always been a dream of yours, and this is a chance to show the world how truly talented you are." As bittersweet as this moment was, it was her moment, and my emotions wouldn't ruin it for her. "I have supported and will *always* support you. And they say absence makes the heart grow fonder, right? You're not going to forget about me when you're famous?"

"Yes." I could hear her soft giggles. "I mean no! I was saying yes to absence making the heart grow fonder. I'd never ever leave you."

"Well, you'll not have time to forget me anyway because I'll visit you every weekend."

"Thank you, handsome." She sighed. "You're just too sweet."

"This is your dream, and I would never stand in the way of you fulfilling it. I love you and I'm proud of you."

"I won't fly out for the next few hours. Do you think you can take the rest of the day off to celebrate with me?"

"Consider it done!" I walked out of the room a second time. "I'll be there in thirty minutes."

"See you soon, baby," she called into the phone as we hung up.

Judy was standing in front of her cubicle with tears in her eyes.

"I know you're gonna miss her, Mr. Banks," she said, reaching up for a hug, patting me on the back like a loving mother.

"Cancel all my appointments for the day," I said.

Then I turned on my heels and headed back toward my office… to face Chloe.

Chapter 23

JANE AND I WORKED tirelessly on a high-profile insider trading case involving CEOs of a number of large corporations in the Boston area. Due to the overwhelming workload and corruption we uncovered, I had to cancel some weekend visits to see London in Peoria, Illinois. By now, she had been working on her commission over there for nearly a month.

London, already making a name for herself, appearing in several well-known art magazines featuring muralists since her departure from Boston, was more than understanding about it all.

On one of those really long nights, still seated in the office as I prepared some documents for an early morning trial, Jane casually walked in through the open door.

"Burning the midnight oil again, huh?" She dropped her briefcase on the floor as she made her way over to the desk. "What are you working on?" Her body moved behind mine, resting lightly against my back in a way that quickened my heartbeat.

"Nothing." I blurted out, closing the folder as I stuffed it inside my backpack. Her fingers were pressing gently on my shoulders. "What are you doing?"

"Relax, Todd!"

She nudged at me with an elbow, pressing her breasts against my back as she pulled her face closer to my ears, her hot breath crashing against them like a tide.

"We have been under a lot of pressure with the upcoming case. There is nothing wrong with getting a massage from a friend." She was still pressing on my shoulders in a comforting manner.

"Do you have an iota of respect for your husband?"

I got up from the desk, shaking whatever unholy thoughts might have crept up in me as I looked at her, not expecting a response.

"You don't really expect me to answer that, do you?" She walked past, picking up her briefcase before turning to flash a smile at me. "Fine! No more special treatment for you. From now on I will keep it strictly professional."

"I hope so." I grabbed my backpack, and we headed out of the office toward the elevator.

****

The elevator opened slowly. Officer Burke, the overnight security guard, was performing his rounds. He would go all the way to the top level, checking out each office on foot, then at the other end of the building, would make his way back down again by elevator every few hours.

"Brother Banks and Attorney Moore!" he yelled, waving his flashlight at our faces, probably to confirm things for himself when we stepped out of the elevator into the dimly lit lobby.

"The two of y'all must be working on a very important case," he said in his heavy Jamaican accent, shaking hands with me.

"What makes you say that?" My eyebrows were raised curiously.

"Because this is the third time this week I caught the two of you leaving outta these parts at the same time. I thank the Lord I'm not a betting man…" he said, walking us to the front door, then unlocking it to let us out, "Otherwise, I would think the two of you were having an affair."

"Now don't go spreading any rumors around here about me or Attorney Banks." Jane's emotionless false laughter echoed through the empty walls of the building.

"The last thing anyone in this office needs to be on is some fabricated office gossip list, with no visible facts." She slipped her arm in mine as she held on tightly. "Now have a good night, Mr. Burke, and remember, married women do not have affairs. We have entanglements."

She said it with an air of finality, dragging my numb feet outside with her as I tried wrapping my head around a rumor of an affair with a married woman.

I escorted Jane to University Place parking garage just a few blocks from the office.

"Can you believe Mr. Burke's ridiculous conspiracy theory about the two of us having a secret affair?" I tossed my head back, laughing for the first time since I heard it. "Isn't that the craziest thing you ever heard? I swear, that man could write good novels."

Stopping abruptly in her tracks, she slipped her arm out of mine, sucking her breath in sharply. Her face was red, brows pulled closer together than usual.

I was choking on my own laughter.

"Crazy?" Her eyes were growing wider by the second. "What's so crazy about it?"

"Because I would never have an affair with a married woman, that's why."

I tried laughing at the seriousness of her expression as I shook my head. "Now, let's get to your car so you can get home to your beautiful family."

Her angry features cooled off.

"You are a man of integrity, Todd." She grabbed my arm again, smiling devilishly at me. "But everyone has a breaking point. Anyway, I suppose I should thank you for being a perfect gentleman and walking me to my car."

She wrapped her arms around my neck and snuggled her face against my cheek, throwing me off balance for a quick second. Sensing I was already yielding to this temptation of hers, she drew me closer to her body, already pressed against the car.

"Can I give you a ride to the train station?" she whispered throatily in my ear, further pressing her warm body against me as I took a deep breath, trying to control myself in the interest of London's trust, at least.

"Thanks…"

The word seemed too heavy for my lips to pronounce but eventually, they did. I slowly broke free from her grip, shifting my backpack onto my shoulder. "But it's not that far away."

"Are you sure?" She hopped into the car, leaving the door still open as she started the engine, "I promise I won't bite."

"I'm good. But thanks." I forced a smile on my face, helping her close the door.

It was already 9:50 p.m. as I dashed out of the parking garage and bee-lined toward the red line to catch the 10:00 p.m. train to Ashmont Station.

Arriving at Harvard Square, it was now 9:57 p.m., leaving just about sufficient time to make it to the train. I reached inside my blazer for my train pass.

Ah. The wallet's inside my backpack.

The backpack slid off of my shoulder, and I reached into the side pocket.

It was 9:59 p.m. as I rushed through the access gate and sped down the long flight of stairs to catch the train, but I was a minute too late; it was already leaving the station.

I let out a frustrated yell, storming out of the Harvard Square train station. Well, now I had to call an Uber instead of waiting around for the next train.

Walking up and down the lonely streets of Harvard Square as I waited for the car, a familiar female voice called out from behind, "Are you sure you don't need a ride?"

"Are you following me?" I headed toward the car, genuinely happy to see her.

"You would be so lucky." She chuckled, unlocking the passenger door. "Get in!"

"But what about the Uber I just called?" I waved my cell phone at her. "The tracker says the driver will be here in fifteen minutes."

"Cancel it, and join me for dinner," she shouted from the car like an obsessed New England Patriots fan. I found myself chuckling at her reaction. "My treat!"

Considering the awkward encounters I'd had with Jane less than an hour ago, going to dinner wasn't the best decision to be made, that I knew.

Throwing caution to the wind, and by extension ignoring my gut for the umpteenth time, I logged into the Uber app to cancel the trip. Tossing my backpack in the backseat of Jane's Porsche, I got in the front passenger seat and fastened my seatbelt.

Minutes later, we pulled into Yvonne's Restaurant and Supper Club, located in the heart of Boston, for dinner and drinks, though the line to get inside already wrapped around the corner.

"This place is wonderful!" Jane whispered, more to herself than me. She leaned from the car and flagged down one of the female customers in the long queue. "How long is the wait?"

"We've been waiting more than forty-five minutes," she shouted. "Probably another thirty or so."

"Thank you." Jane smiled at her, seeing the woman returning to her spot in the queue, with Jane pulling away from the curb.

"Where to now then?"

"Tasty Burger in Back Bay is ten minutes away. I'll call our order in."

"Tasty Burger it is." A wide grin appeared on my face as she laughed lightly.

About an hour later, her car pulled up in front of my house. I alighted with her waiting for me to get inside before speeding off. Once inside, I headed toward the kitchen for a drink, grabbing a Corona out of the refrigerator. Kicking my shoes off on the floor, the couch seemed to beckon.

I was ready to watch SportsCenter, popping the top on the

Corona and reaching for the remote. Well, what bad timing; my cell phone screen lit up.

"Just pulled into your driveway. We need to talk!"

The message came from Chloe.

Chapter 24

THE LATE NIGHTS at the office and early morning court appearances were more mentally and physically exhausting than I could ever have imagined. Chloe showing up the evening before an important court case, uninvited, and without Blake, told me I was in for yet another long night.

Staring blankly at the message, I chugged down the beer, debating whether or not to reply.

Reluctantly, my hand typed out, 'I'll be down in a minute'. Then I sent it, knowing my quiet evening had just flown out through the window.

Deciding to change into something more comfortable, I headed into the bedroom, glad to get rid of my work clothes, slipping into a pair of Boston Celtics shorts and long-sleeved T-shirt. I slipped on my retro Jordans, my mind trying to figure out exactly why Chloe would show up, alone, at my house, at this late hour. A knock at the front door echoed through the house.

"Unbelievable, Chloe! My text said I would be down in a minute," I muttered under my breath.

"I'll be there in a second!" I shouted, hoping she'd hear and exercise a little more patience as I made a mad dash into the laundry room for the bottle of Febreze to freshen up the house.

Returning the bottle to the shelf, I tiptoed to the front door, my hand hovering around the doorknob as I reluctantly opened it.

"What took you so long to answer?" She said it as if believing she possessed some sort of natural right to come in. Almost as though she thought she resided here, with me. Now, she came storming past, headed into the living room—again, as though it was hers.

"Well, hello to you too," I said. "Nice to see you too."

I knew the best thing with any angry woman was to try and ignore the outbursts and just be nice and kind, pleasant and warm company. To be honest, I was the same. It was hard to stay seething at someone who was good to me. This was the approach that hopefully would work on Chloe too. I locked the door, padding away from it, turning on my heels. As I did so, my gaze fell on her as she sat on the chaise lounge, staring at the blank TV screen.

The approach of being nice was not functioning.

Finally, my patience had had enough. I couldn't contain the annoyance factor anymore. She was being plain rude to me—and in my own home too! "Look, what's your problem?" I fired.

I turned the TV on, flipping through channels before landing on SportsCenter. Usually, I would ask the woman what she preferred to watch. I would always put the other person first. Right now, no way. She was insufferable, not deserving any niceness.

"You are my problem," she tossed back, arms folded across her chest. "You should never keep a woman waiting." A frown sat on her face, bedding itself in as if it would stay forever.

Had she thought that would make me fall at her feet? It didn't, driving me further from her.

"Listen, Chloe"—I got up from the couch, headed back to the front door—"you show up to my house uninvited, and then catch an attitude after I send you a text message saying I'll be down in a minute? Whatever crap you're going through, don't take it out on me. I did my best for you today. I could just have not answered, you know. Instead, what did I do? I invited you in, even despite the fact I'm worn out after work and just need a quiet night."

Her eyes seemed as though they might pop out of their sockets.

I opened the door again with a mighty flourish. "Now, stay and be nice or leave and do what the heck you want. Just don't bring that attitude into my home."

She stared as if I had just spoken some form of alien dialect. I held the door wide.

"Come on," I urged. "What's it to be? I have an important case in the morning and I'm tired." I quickly added, looking outside into the lobby, deliberately avoiding her eyes.

"I'm sorry, Todd." A smile flickered across her face, turning into a laugh, "Can I get a hug, please?" Her arms were outstretched, as she stared flirtatiously at me. "You're right. I just behaved like a spoiled brat. I deserve it if you make me go."

"I never said I would make you go. I said it's your choice."

I closed the door again gently, seeking to find the well of calmness in me.

Giving up on receiving a hug from me, she removed her coat, then tossed it on the arm of the chair, revealing black leggings and a matching top that wrapped around her body like a glove.

Slowly, her feet took her toward me as she wrapped her arms around my neck, pressing her tight body against mine. What was it about me lately that there always seemed to be a pair of boobs pressing against me? Had I somehow grown irresistible to women?

"Do you forgive me?" she whispered and pouted.

Taking a few steps back, I raised my hands in a *don't touch me gesture,* still decidedly prickly. "Nothing to forgive," I said bluntly, walking back to the couch. "But just don't take out on me whatever your problems are. I get enough arguments at work. The cases, I mean."

I turned toward her. "So what do you want to talk about?"

"I married the wrong man." She sighed, heading toward me as she plopped down on the couch beside me. "And I can't stop thinking about you."

That again. This is tiring. Exhausting.

"Listen Chloe"—I grabbed her hand, a little rougher than I had intended—"Blake, and not me, is who you should be thinking about. What about for better or worse? Why did you marry Blake if you didn't love him?"

I wanted to yell, but my voice decided to fail me, coming out as a whisper instead.

"Because I couldn't have you, that's why!" she yelled, breaking down in tears. "Marrying your best friend gave me access to you. And I just couldn't be on my own. I was too weak. I had nobody, nobody at all. I was all alone in the world. Do you know what that even feels like?"

I stared. Had she really said that? "You're a pastor. You have God. I thought He was always enough." Ouch. Was that a low blow? But I actually did mean it, did think so. How could she be a pastor and feel so abandoned and alone? It kind of failed to add up.

Now, it cast a shadow over why she had chosen the path she had followed. Had this also been on some kind of a whim? Did she not feel the Lord at her side night and day, no matter what? I hoped so, if not for her own sake then for all of the congregation she counseled. There were, indeed, different shades of crazy and this woman in front of me was definitely a crazy one.

"Are you saying the only reason you married my best friend was because of me?" I repeated her words, slowly, back to her, just to be doubly sure that what I'd heard really had come from her lips. She nodded, wiping away the tears. "I'm afraid so. I just needed you around."

Getting up from the couch, I walked into the kitchen, grabbing the bottle of Jose Cuervo tequila and two shot glasses. I had never known Chloe to drink anything alcoholic, but knew she needed to take the edge off, somehow. Filling the shot glasses with tequila, I handed her one.

She looked up at me, then at the shot glass.

Taking the glass from my grip, she sniffed the black liquor in it. "You're trying to get me drunk, aren't you? I need something a little lighter, please." She handed the drink back to me.

"Sorry. I do have wine." In the kitchen, I retrieved a wine glass and the same bottle of wine I'd planned to bring to her house for dinner nearly two months ago.

"Here you go." I poured wine into the glass, handing it over to her. She took a sip.

"This is good!" She smacked her lips, gulping the contents down almost immediately.

Helping herself to another glass, which she also gulped down, she smiled from ear to ear. Occasional chuckles fell from her lips. The third glass of wine was, however, the end of her chuckles. Her eyelids shut tight, falling into a deep sleep.

Waking her up for her to drive home became a terrible idea. No way should she drive, and I should have considered this before giving the alcohol.

I dashed up the stairs to grab a blanket from the linen closet.

Upon returning, the couch was empty. My heart sank almost immediately.

"Chloe?" I shouted, frantically searching around the living room for any signs of her.

Afraid that she might have driven herself home, I searched outside to make sure her drunk behind hadn't stupidly left. Her car, still parked in the driveway, turned into a comforting reassurance.

Shortly, my eyes landed on her lying in the middle of my bed, curled in the fetal position. An annoyance and yet a relief too, oddly, not wishing to be culpable for a vehicle accident.

I covered her with the blanket I didn't even realize my hands were still holding, then I closed the bedroom door and headed back into the living room for another much-needed drink.

Reaching for the bottle of Jose Cuervo tequila, the ringtone of my phone blared, causing me to almost spill what was in the glass. My heart raced even faster now: the caller was Blake.

Well, of course it would be. It seemed that whenever his wife was missing or tied up on the phone, he immediately thought of me. He suspected I would be the one keeping her away. Again.

Slowly, I dropped the bottle of tequila and shot glass on the table, reaching to answer.

My finger tapped the green button against all better judgment. "Hello?"

"I'll be there in fifteen minutes, so unlock the door."

This was no friendly voice.

PART FIVE

HUNTER

Chapter 25

AUNT JANE EXCITEDLY shared childhood pictures of me with Harper, and that was the moment I chose to exit, heading to join Destiny on the couch. She was watching the Boston Celtics game on TNT as my brain conjured up a way to escape this boring dinner party charade.

"Want to get out of here?" I smiled, a nefarious twinkle in my eye.

She turned her head toward me.

"What are you up to, Hunter?" She had a raised eyebrow, a soft chuckle escaping her lips.

"This!" I flashed my driver's license in her face, a proud smile on my expression.

Having just completed my driver's education class a month earlier and having also passed the driver's test, Destiny and I were just moments away from being free of the loonies in this house. All that remained was the need to get the key to Uncle Lee's truck.

"Yes!" Her eyes lit up. She clapped as I dashed out of the living room, beelining toward Uncle Lee's bedroom to execute my plan. Slowly pushing open the door, my gaze fell on Uncle Lee stretched out on the bed, reading the Art of War. I dragged my feet inside the room.

"Excuse me, Uncle Lee!" My heart was slamming against my ribcage as I swallowed hard. The moment was intense, but I was ready.

He stared up at me, probably wondering why I had left the dinner party. "Is everything okay?" He dropped the book he was reading, his way of saying I had his undivided attention.

"I hate to ask, but…" I was trying to be careful and properly scrutinize each word before they escaped through my mouth.

"...but it's getting late, and Destiny needs a ride home. Mind if I borrow your truck? I promise, I'll not be long."

A sneaky smile said, *I know that trick, lad.* It widened across his face. "My keys are over there." He pointed at the dresser. "Just make sure your aunt knows what you're doing."

I was already halfway to the door, uninterested in his advice.

"And one last thing," he called, causing me to stop in my tracks. "She better be worth it."

"She is!" I smiled, more to myself than him, heading through the open door before he had a chance to change his mind. Dangling Uncle Lee's keys in front of Destiny, I laughed softly.

"Got them!"

"Wow! How did you do it?" She stared at me with a raised eyebrow, trying hard to mask her own smiles against the wishes of her eyes.

"Do what?" I paced back and forth in the living room, occasionally poking my head in the kitchen to spy on Aunt Jane and Harper, now playing UNO at the kitchen table.

"How did you convince your uncle to hand over his car keys, silly?"

"I told him you needed a ride home."

"Hunter James!" She waved her hand with a dismissive

gesture, chuckling even louder as she tried muffling the sound with her hand. "What am I going to do with you?"

Ignoring the rhetorical question, I watched Aunt Jane pour the last few drops of wine into her glass, just two sips of wine away from officially being drunk.

"I got it!" I turned abruptly, grabbing Destiny by the shoulder, shaking her gently. She gave me a confused stare. "Grab your things."

"What do you have?" She tugged the back of my shirt. I turned toward the kitchen.

"Just follow my lead," I said, leading the walk into the kitchen, looking guilty as sin itself.

"What have the two of you been up to?" Harper asked in an accusatory tone, mean mugging both Destiny and me.

Getting up from the table, Aunt Jane grabbed another bottle of wine from the cabinet.

"Yeah," she slurred almost drunkenly, taking a seat back down. "The two of you have been awfully quiet. And where is your Uncle Lee? I haven't seen him since he gobbled down my good ol' sweet pumpkin pie."

"Maybe you poisoned him," I heard escaping my mouth before I could reel the words in. Fortunately for me, Aunt Jane only snickered, far too inebriated to get cross with me. Now, she set off giggling as if we shared some kind of secret joke between us, that she wanted Uncle dead. God, I so hoped not, though at times, it sure came across that way—that she detested him.

Standing, Harper's feet took her in circles around me as though I was a dead cactus on a windy road. Stopping in front of me, her cold stares alternated between Destiny and me. "Sure the two of you aren't hiding anything?"

What was it with this lunatic?

First, she squirted me on the first day of school, hugged and kissed me during the basketball game, crashed the dinner party, and now she was questioning me as though we were dating.

"What time are your parents picking you up?" I smiled smugly, sure this would get a rise out of her. "It's getting late."

"They'll be here in five minutes." Her stares were digging holes into me as she stomped away to the living room, Destiny and I following slowly behind.

Aunt Jane, clearly impaired, stumbled into the living room and fell on the couch, her loud snores echoing through the room almost immediately. Harper's cell phone, however, rang a few minutes after Aunt Jane started her journey into dreamland.

Harper picked up, having a really short conversation with whoever it was.

"Thank you for a lovely dinner, Mrs. Moore." She leaned down and gave sleeping Aunt Jane a hug. "My parents are here."

Turning to Destiny and me, she forcefully grabbed the back of my neck.

Then she planted a kiss on my cheek.

"The next time you ignore me and spend time with that loser, Destiny, will be the last time we ever speak. But since I like you and think you're cute, you get a one-time pass. Don't let it happen again." She said it all in one breath. She grabbed a handful of my butt and squeezed.

"Good night, everyone. Ciao!" She waved at Destiny, who nodded in understanding.

Grimacing with pain, I begrudgingly escorted her to the door, bidding a polite goodbye.

Aunt Jane hadn't moved an inch from the position she was in a few minutes ago, as she drooled on the side of the couch. This was the once-in-a-lifetime chance to make our move.

"Are you ready?" I signaled to Destiny, already standing behind me.

"Okay, Aunt Jane." I rubbed the back of her arm gently, unsure if really ready to face the consequences of my rebellion later on.

SECRETS ENEMY

"I'm going to take Destiny home now. If it's okay with you, I may stay awhile. Talk to you soon," I whispered from the door, afraid of waking her by going any closer.

Scurrying out of the house, locking the door behind us, we hopped into Uncle Lee's truck, the sound of our laughter traveling through the night.

Chapter 26

"I HAVE TO WARN YOU…" Destiny reached over and turned off the radio, the blank look in her unseeing eyes telling me whatever she was about to share was more than important.

"You are about to enter into a world that you have only seen on TV." She chuckled softly, her face inches away from mine.

"Bring it on!" I stared at her for a quick second before focusing on the road, turning onto Blue Hill Avenue, trying not to laugh. Did she want me to show fear? I honestly wasn't afraid of the world she was speaking of, even though I hadn't seen it yet. To be able to survive living with a controlling Aunt, like Aunt Jane, was an automatic ticket to survival anywhere else.

Moreover, driving through a lake of fire meant nothing to me, as long as I got to spend every minute, alone, with Destiny. Yes, she was worth it all, even my death.

"Okay, tough guy!" She nodded slowly, a smirk finding its way to her beautiful face as I stole yet another glance. "My crazy uncle and his friends are at the house now. I'm sure they'll be delighted to meet you."

"I can't wait to meet them." A wide grin was on my face. She chuckled even louder, a part of me hoping this wasn't a 'biting off more than I could chew' kind of situation.

"The more the merrier," I whispered. "It'll be fine." It was loud enough for her to hear, but in actual fact, was really just to reassure myself of my own safety.

Sitting with all her glory and magnificence in the night sky, the moon watched our car turn onto River Road, where Destiny's house was located.

"You have reached your destination," the female voice from the GPS system said softly as I stopped in front of the compound, peering in to see any form of imminent danger.

"Pull into the driveway where my uncle and his friends are playing basketball."

Her soft voice came out, followed by her pointing fingers.

Looking over my shoulder, my gaze met her sneaky grin. The kind of grin that said, 'welcome to my world', but I wasn't going to be fazed by just a mere grin.

Unfastening her seatbelt, she rolled the window down, waving at the men in front of us. "Get out of the driveway before my friend runs you over."

"What are you doing?" I said via clenched teeth, palms suddenly too sweaty for the wheel.

Slowly, I pulled the truck forward, nearly hitting one of the guys even at that pace, heart pounding as I looked over at Destiny. She didn't seem affected by what just happened.

It was then I knew, for a fact, that I was about eating my own words.

Goodbye to Mr. Brave Guy.

"Fair warning, tough guy." She smiled at my face, opening the truck door, climbing out.

Standing behind the closed door, her hands were on the window. "Whatever you do, do not look the big one in the eyes."

"But he's staring at me." My voice came out shaky, ignoring my instructions of not showing fear in front of Destiny.

Walking up the driveway with Destiny leading the way, my hands trembled by my side as I tried masking the fear stubbornly hugging my feet.

Lowering my head, I avoided direct eye contact with the biggest human I had ever seen, shadowing Destiny's every move, focusing on the back of her black and white Nike Blazers.

Everything was going as planned, turning left or right only when her Nike Blazers did, until fate decided otherwise, sending me tripping over my untied shoelace. Struggling against falling flat on my face, I barreled right into Destiny, sending her flying across the driveway into the arms of the one person I was desperately trying to avoid: Goliath.

Gently moving Destiny aside, he grabbed the front of my shirt with just one hand and pinned me to the side of the house. "Someone has careless feet," he shouted over his shoulder.

The others cheered him on.

"It was an accident," I squealed and tried to break free from his tight grip, my eyes wandering toward Destiny just standing with the others, smiling.

Do something before he kills me! I yelled at Destiny in my head, watching my life flash before me like a corny reality show. Just when I thought things couldn't get any worse, I felt a drop of warm dew coursing down my right leg; it was pee. The dime-sized wet spot in the center of my pants glared back as I prayed earnestly for my bullies not to notice it as well. My prayers were answered as Destiny's voice broke through the chaos, saving me from further doom.

"Let him go!" She parted the small circle, yanking me out of his grasp.

"This is the reason I never bring anyone from school home." For someone who'd been smiling just a minute ago, it was a really impressive transition, that I must admit.

"Are you okay?" She slipped her hand into mine, leading me safely inside the house.

"It was a joke, niece," the big guy yelled after us, the men's laughter ringing in my ears as they headed back to their basketball game as though nothing had happened.

"You sure you're okay?" she asked a second time, her eyes holding some form of guilt.

"Yeah, I'm fine." I lied; it was the logical response to give to the question asked.

"They were just playing, right?" I forced a chuckle, though I could feel my heart slamming against my rib cage.

Standing on the porch still holding hands, the events of a few minutes ago replayed in my head. I suddenly felt like a coward for squealing like a pig in front of her. Just maybe I wasn't as tough as I'd thought, but the one thing I knew for sure was that Destiny was right.

Her world was unlike anything I could ever have imagined. It left me with this gut feeling that meeting this family of hers would change me for the rest of my life.

Chapter 27

THANKFULLY, BEING OBEDIENT to Aunt Jane's choice of outfit paid off, as my name would have surely skyrocketed to the top of the school's gossip list if I had worn the gray sweatsuit I'd had in mind. Our elders did smell danger from a mile away if I'm allowed to say that.

Before meeting with other members of Destiny's family, I scurried into the bathroom to make sure that pee was the only foreign liquid to embarrassingly leave my body.

Unzipping my pants, a sigh of relief exhaled. My new boxers hadn't been soiled.

I leaned my left hand against the wall in front of me, as I took a leak.

"Ahhhhhhhh."

"Hunter?" Destiny called out, banging on the bathroom door as the sound of the doorknob being turned filled my ears. "What are you doing in there, and why are you moaning?"

Quickly, I zipped up my pants, flushing the toilet and turning on the faucet. "I'll be out in a minute." *Where is the soap?* I plunged my hands under the cold water, rubbing them together.

Turning the knob a second time, the door pushed open. She remained standing on the other side of the door with her hands on hips. "Are you sure you're okay?"

Were this girl and her crazy family for real?

First, I'd been nearly assaulted by her uncle who'd literally scared the piss out of me, and written it all off as a joke. Now, she was trying to barge in on my bathroom session, still saying it was a 'show of concern'. What was I even getting myself into?

Perhaps Harper, and not Destiny, was the safer bet after all. Though she was crazy too.

Walking out of the bathroom toward Destiny, the girl effortlessly made me doubt my own insecurities and fears, unable to help the grin on my face. She stared with a raised eyebrow;

it was kinda cute, I must admit. "What?" I shrugged, a soft chuckle sounding.

Her strict expression refused to be broken.

Suddenly grabbing my wrist, she pulled me down the long hallway like a dog on a leash.

"I want to introduce you to my mother." She said it plainly, not giving me any time to respond, or maybe my response wasn't actually needed.

A few seconds later, we were standing in the entranceway of the kitchen where a woman, with a striking resemblance to the actress Gabrielle Union, was loading plates into the dishwasher. With just one glance, it was obvious where Destiny got her stunningly good looks.

"Mom, this is Hunter James, the friend I was telling you about the other day." Destiny was already standing beside her mom, leaving me in the entranceway, my face turning red.

Destiny deemed me worthy to talk about with her mother! Wow! Maybe, just maybe, she liked me as much as I liked her, and clearly, the stars were aligning.

"So, you're the superstar basketball player that my daughter's been raving about?"

She closed the dishwasher, walking from behind the counter

toward me, perhaps of course to properly welcome me with a wide smile.

I stretched out my arm ready for a handshake, and she pulled me into a warm embrace.

Shocked would be a grave understatement of how I felt, though not resisting the comfort her hug brought. She smelled like freshly picked roses with a hint of strawberries and brown sugar.

"It's nice to meet you, Mrs. Clarke."

My voice was barely a whisper, inaudible to even my ears.

This would be my first time, since we'd arrived in Massachusetts, that I'd have spent time with a family other than my own.

"It's Ms. Clarke." Her soft voice politely corrected me; she was still smiling sweetly.

Why had I assumed Destiny's mother was married? She wasn't wearing a wedding ring, but as usual, I always had to put my foot in my mouth.

The doorbell ringing arrested any apology I was cooking up in my head.

"It was nice meeting you, son." She hugged me a second time, respectfully excusing herself to attend to the door.

A few seconds with Destiny's mother and she'd treated me with so much love and kindness, unlike her uncle. Maybe her world wasn't that bad after all.

As we stood in the middle of the kitchen, my mind took me down memory lane, reminding me of Uncle Lee's famous words about family, that one bad apple could spoil the rest. In the case of Destiny's family, her uncle was, well, let's just say his fat butt was rotten to the core.

For the next ten minutes or so, Destiny gave me a tour of her beautiful home, showing me each room, decorated like a show home.

I still didn't know what Destiny's mother did for a living, but based on the size of their home and how beautifully decorated it was, it had to be important.

The tour ended with Destiny leading me downstairs with food and drinks.

Soon, we were in a room with a row of wide customized leather New England Patriots home theater chairs right in the middle, facing a wall on which was mounted the largest flat-screen TV I had ever seen, Boston Celtics and Red Sox championship banners hanging on each side of it.

To the left were matching treadmills and a Tonel Smart Home Gym. The back of this amazing room wasn't left out, accommodating a classic bar and barstools. The ceiling chose to outshine them all, adorned with surround sound speakers, causing my jaw to drop, literally. This was definitely that place you'd hate leaving; it was absolute heaven.

My eyes had been fixed on the television screen for God knew how long, scared to even blink else I'd miss a tide-changing moment of this game. The Celtics were already ahead of the Knicks by twenty points, and I was anxiously waiting to see if the Knicks could bounce back.

The screen suddenly went off.

Looking over at Destiny to find answers, my gaze fell upon the remote in her firm grip.

"What are you doing?" I reached for it to turn the game back on, but she was quicker than I had hoped, tucking it safely beside her where she was sure I wouldn't reach.

Just a few minutes ago, she had asked me to make myself at home, and now she'd turned off the TV right in the middle of an important game. This was just straight-up BS.

"The night of the game…" She looked me squarely in the eyes, following my wandering gaze. "What happened?"

Ignoring her question, I reached for the remote a second time. "Can you please turn the game back on?"

"Not until you tell me why you were crying that night." Have

I told you she was adamantly stubborn? Yes, and today was not a day to condone her stubbornness.

"Nothing," I heard myself yell against my own wish, folding my arms across my narrow chest, staring holes into the dark TV screen.

I could already feel the tears threatening to break free as my mind wandered back to the answers of the questions she had asked. Taking a deep breath, I wiped my left eye with the back of my hand, preventing any loose tears from dropping.

"Hunter..." she called softly, her hand grabbing the back of my head as she pushed herself closer, kissing me softly on the edge of my mouth, "I like you a lot. Your secret is safe with me."

Completely caught off guard, I said, "W-what was th-that for?" I didn't usually stutter, but the words just would not emerge correctly.

Twice, I had been kissed without my consent, but this felt surreal, and I honestly wanted it to last, wanted to taste her lips completely, and not just from the side.

"It's no secret that we are attracted to one another." She smiled bashfully at me. "You're also attracted to me, right?" Maybe she realized it was better to ask than to assume.

"Very much." I didn't spare a second to silence as the kryptonite effect she possessed over me had already weakened my defenses.

I was more than ready to share my darkest secret.

Chapter 28

"WHERE SHOULD I START?"

"Wherever you feel safest."

She pushed herself closer into me, squeezing my hand tightly, oblivious to the hauntingly dark secret I was about to share for the first time in a really long while.

"Mom was in the kitchen preparing dinner." I started my tale with a heavy sigh. "My older brothers, Jason and David asked if I wanted to play hide and seek, something the three of us did almost every night, more like a family tradition!

Jason's hiding spot was under someone's bed, and It was always the first place I'd look. David's hiding place was in Dad's office and finding him wasn't so easy. Dad's office was supposed to be off limits, but he hid there anyway."

My gaze met with Destiny's tender stare, which urged me on.

"My favorite hiding spot was inside Mom's antique armoire, and my brothers were both too big to fit inside it, so they'd never think to look for me there. But Mom had warned everyone in the house to stay away from her priceless armoire, but I never listened."

A smile came creeping up my face, Destiny's grip growing tighter, warming my cold hands.

"Anyway, from my hideaway, I watched Mom preparing dinner in the kitchen. Dad was in his office down the hall, getting ready for a court proceeding as the doorbell rang.

"I still remember vividly each and every conversation that fateful evening; do you want to hear all of it?" I looked over at Destiny who nodded slowly, probably getting afraid she might end up hearing something she wasn't brave enough to bear.

"My mom leaned back, looking down the hallway as she shouted toward Dad's office, 'Honey! Can you answer the door?'

"He shouted, 'Are you expecting guests?' From the tone his voice held, it was obvious he didn't like the interruption.

"She said, 'No, but you know my brother Lee always shows up when I make pot roast.' Mom was still focused on the delicious meal she was making.

"He replied, 'Whatever happened to calling first? Damn freeloader!' Dad's tone wasn't so friendly. He was really bothered by Uncle Lee's surprise visits. He had been for a while.

"From inside the armoire, I saw Mom's face in a frown, and she dashed from the kitchen, bumping the ancient piece of furniture with me inside as she passed by. Now, she was outside Dad's office, and she said, 'You know we're all he has since Mom and Dad passed away. It's been a few years now, but he still relies on us, sweetie. Take it easy on him, okay?'

"Dad appeared in the doorway, taking Mom's hand.

"He smiled at her, leaning in for a kiss. As a kid, I'd have screamed that it was gross but now, I miss seeing those gross moments."

A tear escaped, Destiny's diligent hand catching it before it fell to my cheeks.

"Mom was one of the only people I'd ever seen break through Dad's defenses. Maybe it was because she was a psychiatrist, or maybe it was just the way she looked at him that softened him up. Either way, it worked every time. Don't forget, I was still safely hidden in the armoire."

Destiny nodded to show she was understanding the tale.

"From my hiding spot, I heard my brothers' footsteps approaching. Then, 'Where could he be? He has to be here somewhere.'

"That was Jason, just twelve years old and already nearly six feet tall, the best middle school athlete in the county. He was already excelling in both track and basketball!

"David joined in next, our eldest brother. 'Yeah but where is he? That's the question!' They were really enjoying hunting me down. But David was a lot different from Jason; without Jason's athletic gifts, he'd made a name for himself as the neighborhood tyrant.

"Scared of being discovered, I froze inside the armoire, their footsteps crossing the living room and coming right near my hiding spot! Holding my breath, I could hear them rustling around, searching for me. But those weren't the only sounds. There were these weird muffled voices coming from the front door. Suddenly, a thud came from the entryway and there was, like, this horrible loud scream. Jason's and David's footsteps were running from the room.

"Not even a minute later, their yells and screams came as well, and three more thuds.

"My little mind could only repeat over and over, *what's happening? Oh no, oh no, oh no.*"

Taking a long breather, I exhaled as long and calm as I could, preparing for the next part.

Destiny was tapping gently on my hands, still safely in her grip.

"I found myself peeking through the crack around the armoire door again, craning my neck to see into the living room, and to my horror, there were two really huge guys dressed in all black, with matching Batman masks. It was surreal, Destiny, you know? Because there they were in these Batman masks which you'd normally find funny. There was *nothing* funny, believe me.

"It was like staring death in the face. Really. I just knew what this was. One of them had a gun, and it was pointed at Dad. I could see him all tied up in a chair with blood running down the side of his head. My stomach knotted. I shoved the back of my hand against my mouth to keep myself from screaming or being sick. Who were they, and what did they want? These were questions I had no answers to. But I was pretty sure they were here to kill us all. *Kill* is too mild a word. Slaughter us all. That's a lot more accurate. Sorry for the detail but it's how it was.

"The worst part was hearing Dad pleading, 'Please, let my wife and kids go! They have nothing to do with this!" It was almost a whine, like an animal caught in a trap. He stared at the floor.

"Following Dad's gaze to the edge of the doorway, I could see three pairs of feet, Mom's, David's, and Jason's. Were they okay? They weren't moving or making any noise. Surely Dad would get us all out of this. *Yeah, Dad will get us out,* said the voice in my head, before saying, *no, he won't. He can't. We're all dying.* And I was sure they'd find me too. These thoughts ran through my psyche, blind confidence in my father being my only reassurance.

"A hopeless, pointless confidence in him. Every kid, especially a boy, thinks his dad is a superhero, you know? This was the moment I realized my dad just wasn't one. That he was nothing special in that regard. He was just a man, just a dad like anyone else's. Broke my heart.

"One of the men spoke then, saying, 'Go get the tape to shut this fool up'. He motioned to his partner, who brought this big spool of a wide gray tape over straight away.

"'I got the tape, boss,' he said, and he was excited. It was disgusting, turned my guts.

"'Then you best muzzle this loudmouth before I end him.'

"'No problem, boss.' Pulling his arm back, he punched Dad right in the jaw with a straight right and Dad's head really whiplashed with the blow, then sagged to the side. I wanted to scream, cry, whimper. But I couldn't do any of those things because—"

"Shh, I know," sweet Destiny said, sensing my distress, caressing my hair and the side of my face with a hand. "You don't need to go on. I know what hell this is. Please, stop. If I'd known it'd be anything like this, you know I wouldn't have asked. I've been horrible."

She started to cry, just small sobs. The guilt had grabbed a hold of her. I wanted to cry too, but not for me, not for the suffering I had gone through. For Destiny. She was an empathic angel.

But I wouldn't stop talking about those hideous events because in some bizarre way, it seemed this might be cathartic. This could turn out to be good for me. God knew, I'd been holding it, holding it, holding it… for so long that it was eating me away from the insides, and some nights, I'd jolt awake and dash off to throw up, then struggle to get to sleep again. Maybe by sharing, maybe it'd be like Mom always used to say: 'A problem shared is a problem halved'.

I hoped so. Hope was all I had. So, I reassured Destiny and continued.

"So, this guy demanded to the other, 'What the hell are you doing?'

"And the first one said, 'You told me to shut him up, boss.'

"The one who had landed the punch replied, 'I meant with the tape, you stupid idiot.'

"'Oh! Sorry, boss.' He was laughing, quickly tearing off a piece of tape and he slapped it noisily across Dad's mouth. How was Dad going to help us all—or himself—now?"

Destiny had cuddled extremely close to me, and I could oddly feel her gaze directly on my lips and see the wetness in her eyes, though she tried masking it with a half-smile for my sake.

"I still remember swallowing the lump in my throat as I did the only thing I could think of: I prayed. Mom had made it a point of duty to teach me that God would be there to help those who couldn't help themselves, and that was us right now. So I prayed and pleaded, 'Dear God, please save my family from these bad men, and hurry. Amen.' I whispered it, maybe audible or maybe silent to myself, I don't know. But I know I was shutting my eyes tight, clasping my hands.

"'Now, before I end your worthless life, you piece-of-crap attorney, I want you to see what happens to people who mess with me,' the boss man—that's what I refer to him as—said to Dad, as he reached down and yanked Mom to her feet.

"Mom's face was flooded with tears as the big man held her by the hair to stand her right there in front of Dad, in the living room doorway. 'Hand me one of those pillows,' He demanded from his sidekick, waving his gun toward the couch.

"'Here you go, boss.'

"'Say goodbye to your family.'

"The man leered at Dad, placing the pillow against Mom's face and, without warning, he pulled the trigger. Her body just collapsed sideways with a heavy thud, slumping to the floor.

"My little mind reeled as Dad's muffled groans reached the armoire where I hid. His face was flooded with tears as he struggled with his tied limbs to go to his family, pleading with the men to spare the rest of us, his kids. I wondered if he was also asking himself where I was.

"I squeezed my eyes closed, trying to shut it all out. But this wasn't a nightmare. It was real. There was no way to shut out something like this.

"'Hey boss, can I get a piece of the action?' one of the men asked. 'Can I do something?'

"'Sure, why not?'

"The big man's voice filled my ears, and my eyes popped

back open to see the sidekick grabbing David off the floor. Unlike Mom, David remained silent as he was pulled to his feet.

"Brandishing a sharp silvery knife, the sidekick grinned widely. The only thing I can be thankful for is that he was really fast—like, so fast you almost couldn't catch what he was doing.

"He reached around and quick as a flash, slit David's throat, dropping him to the floor beside Mom. A fountain of blood had spurted high to the ceiling and down the wall, then it went more to normal bleeding and overflowed, pooling on the floor. I don't think he'd have felt it.

"Then, I remember trying not to, but I could smell the iron tang at the same time as I tasted the salt of my own tears, silently pouring down my face.

"I didn't want to continue watching my family being killed, but couldn't stop either. Then Jason, still on the floor, twisted violently as he was hit by a bullet from the boss man's gun.

"'Any last words, mister hot shot attorney?' The boss man ripped the tape off Dad's mouth, and the man was really grinning, obscene. I can't help but wonder now, how he enjoyed killing a mother and her kids. I mean, he'd obviously seen evil like that maybe as he was growing up. I dunno. But I'd like to think there was some rational reason for why he wound up so warped.

"'You will burn in hell for this,' was the last thing my father ever voiced.

"'Doubtful. I don't believe in hell. But you can go there for me if you think it exists. Then come back and let me know what it's like just in case I want to reserve a spot. Right?'

"He raised his gun once more, aiming for the center of Dad's forehead. He pulled the trigger one final time, Dad's body jerking for some seconds. And then he went limp. I…"

Destiny's finger on my lips arrested the other words as she wiped her face of many tears.

A few seconds later, her arms were wrapped around my neck as she buried her face in my shoulder. She smelled like fresh flowers on a summer day, and I was tempted to pick one.

Instead, we sat there, entrapped in each other's hold. The tears I'd been careful not to show streamed down my face. My hand found its way around her waist, holding onto her tighter.

"Hunter?" She tilted her head, gazing up. "Kiss me!"

This was it! The moment I had been waiting for since the first day of school was finally here, and I was going to grab it with both hands although it was a sad moment of connection.

Closing my eyes, I braced myself for the kiss of a lifetime.

The basement door suddenly cracked open, loud footsteps on the wooden stairs coming.

Shoving Destiny to the side before we got caught locking lips in her house, I grabbed the remote from the cupholder, mashing the power button.

Seconds later, two well-dressed guys in black suits and dark sunglasses walked in.

"Uncle Henry!" Destiny leaped out of her chair into the arms of one. She hugged him.

"Who is he?" he asked, looking over her shoulder at me. The devilish look in his eyes was way more frightening than a horror movie, and I found myself deliberately looking away.

Deciding it was courteous to greet an elder, I quietly walked from behind the couch, hoping I didn't crap on myself, stretching out my hand.

"Hi," I swallowed hard the lump in my throat. "I'm Hunter James."

Why was every male in her family so enormous and intimidating?

"Who's winning the game?" he asked.

Then he walked past, ignoring my outstretched hand, plopping down on my chair.

Peering over at Destiny through lifeless eyes, I smiled timidly at her.

"Do something," I mouthed.

"Don't be so rude, Uncle Henry."

She grabbed my arm, dragging me over to the two of them, who had now made themselves comfortable watching the game. "This is the boy I was telling you about."

"What boy?" Uncle Henry leaned forward, snatching the remote out of my loose grip. "Refresh my memory," he said absentmindedly, stretching himself out on the chair.

Standing in the middle of the living room, beads of sweat already forming on my forehead, I spotted the other guy watching me intently, as though I had stolen something belonging to him.

"Do I know you?" He pinned me with his eyes.

"Um, I don't think so."

"Uncle Sanchez, will you leave him alone?" Destiny interrupted, turning her attention from Uncle Henry to the second man. "He's not even from Boston."

Reaching out, he said, "Oh yeah!" He grabbed my hand and pulled me close. "But that conversation's not over. I'm sure I know you from somewhere. I just can't put my finger on it."

"Leave him alone," Henry chimed in as my heart slammed harder and faster against my ribs. "If he's a friend of my niece, he's cool with me." He had a smile as scary as his frown, standing up as he wrapped me in a bear hug. "So you are the superstar basketball player who's going to lead Cloud Valley to its first city championship, huh?"

"I hope so." I exhaled and smiled, a little more comfortable than a few minutes ago, but Sanchez still had his eyes on me as I adjusted in my skin.

"Where are you from?" His voice coursed through the room.

"Peoria"—the name almost rolled off my tongue—"Peoria, Illinois."

"No way!" He yelled it out, a chuckle emerging, causing every other person in the room to look at him. "I knew you looked familiar. Is your father a lawyer?"

I nodded. He peered over at Henry, whispering something in his ear. Their faces turned pale.

"That's not him." Henry shook his head, sizing me up. "No way."

"My father is dead," I said softly, trying to allay whatever misconception they might be having about me.

"How did he die?"

"My family was murdered when I was six. I live with my aunt and uncle now."

Turning to Henry, who still stared on with widened eyes, "We have to go," Sanchez said.

"But why? The game's almost over." I wasn't understanding

any of this drama, but couldn't be responsible for them leaving just minutes after arriving.

"It was nice to meet you, Hunter." Sanchez tightened his fist by his side, forcing out final words. Even those seemed uncomfortable. "We'll see you again soon." Something about those words made me tremble, juddering, filled with anxiety.

He led the way up the stairs. They disappeared into the house.

"They seemed nice enough." I smiled at Destiny, who stared with just as much confusion.

"They are." She tried shaking off the mixed emotions her uncles had left as she wrapped her arms around my neck again. "Now, where were we?"

A naughty smirk sat on her face. She stared deep into my eyes.

PART SIX

TODD

Chapter 29

STORMING IN LIKE a member of the SWAT team as I jerked the bedroom door open, my gaze fell on Chloe, peacefully asleep on the king-sized bed, snoring very loudly.

"Get up!" I violently shook the side of the bed. "Blake called, and he's on his way here."

"I told you. Blake's out of town on business," she whispered, staring up at me through her half-opened eyelids.

"No. He just called."

I grunted my frustration, hoping somehow she'd understand the urgency of the situation, "And if you are not out of here in the next five minutes, someone is either getting arrested or dying an early death tonight." I pulled the comforter down from her sleeping body.

Choosing to deliberately ignore me, or maybe it was just the drowsy effects of the wine she had, she grabbed the hem of the plush down comforter and pulled it back over her head.

This girl was intent on going back to sleep.

Hell! What now? I cursed at my panic-stricken self, darting back into the living room, opening the mini blinds to check the surroundings for any signs of Blake's car; there was none.

Plopping down on the couch, the realization of the rubber finally meeting the road hit me like a heavy blow to the jaw. Was there any way out of this mess?

My really pressured, time-limiting thinking ended with just two options to consider. These were to either tell the truth, whatever that was, or to whoop Blake's ass and go to jail for assault.

Neither of these options appealed to me, so instead, I kicked my shoes off on the living room floor, deciding it was best to take a short nap just before the war began. Stretching myself out on the couch with my eyes closed, my wretched phone blared its ringtone.

With the speed of light, I reached for it. Sure enough, it was Blake.

"Hello?" I could barely hear my own voice, but somehow hoped he did. My heart leaped and danced, fearful, agitated, horror stricken at the knowledge of what was to come.

"Change of plans, man." His tone was blunt. My vitals slowly returned to normal, "I decided not to come after all."

What a relief! There is, indeed, a God!

"Cool." I uttered in the most casual of ways, tucking away the relief from my voice as I got up from the couch, headed into the kitchen, bouncing internally as though I had won the lottery.

"I have to be at court in the morning anyway. Maybe we can have lunch tomorrow?" I offered, maybe in complete sincerity, I can't really say.

But an awkward silence was the response he deemed to give.

"Tell me the truth, TB." His voice was back, lifeless though and rid of every flicker of sarcasm. Whatever this truth was that he wanted to know, it must be really important. It sent my poor heart back into the most terrible palpitations.

"What do you mean?" I was trying to think of the possible truth he would demand from me.

"How long have we been friends?"

"Since freshman year of college. Why, what gives?" I replied, not sparing a second to silence, his loud sigh filling my ears for the umpteenth time.

"Is my wife there?"

The question sent daggers straight at my heart, a lump appearing in my throat. Words refused to form in my mouth as I scratched the back of my head, tapping my foot on the floor.

"Why would your wife be here when she is married to you?"

I had just taken the coward's way out. Just like Peter on the night of Jesus' betrayal, I heard a rooster crow, or maybe it was just my guilt allowing me to hear things.

"She is there, isn't she?" His voice was laced with a deep sadness that only poked at my guilt all the more. Was Blake crying?

Tell him the truth! My guilt yelled at my ears, but like the first time, I still didn't know what the truth was, and so decided to keep on with the lie. It was obviously mere speculation on Blake's part. He had no way to know that Chloe was showing up at my place. And I was torn; as my friend, wasn't it the correct thing to tell him? To support the man I'd known forever?

On the other hand, it would be betraying Chloe. A part of me said: *it's her business. Hers to tell if she wants to. Not yours.*

"Like I told you. Chloe isn't here."

"You lying, no good mother—" He stopped himself halfway through, probably realizing it was unchristian to curse. "I know she's there. Want to know how I know?"

"How?" I heard myself say when my mouth was supposed

to again be saying it was impossible. Now, the notion of Blake acting out on mere suspicions flew out through the window, my bruised heart slamming yet more against my rib cage.

"Because I put a tracking device on her phone, you no good bastard."

His voice suddenly clouded with his loud sobs. I stood motionless in the kitchen, staring blankly into empty space. It would be regarded as a foolish thing to say that I was lying to protect our friendship. But it was now, that friendship was still far from over, so I hoped.

Blake's weak and vulnerable side wasn't a pleasant thing to see, or to be more specific, hear. He bawled into the phone, my guilt tugging at my heart for causing this irreparable damage.

"You got it all wrong…" I said softly, taking a seat at the kitchen table, as his crying gradually died down. "She just showed up out of the blue, man. Ask her. I didn't even want to let her in, and we had a disagreement over it. I mean if I'd been scared of you finding out, why didn't I then push her out of my place as soon as I heard you were coming over? It's because I'm not at fault.

"I'll tell you why I also didn't make her leave. Because it was all her decision to stop by here. Nothing to do with me. It's *her* battle to have with you. Her own decisions. I'm sorry for not telling you the truth earlier. But as God is real, I promise you I'm telling the truth. I was trying to get her out, sending her to you. Honestly, ask her. I promise you from the bottom of my—"

"I don't want to hear your promises, TB. You lied again and again, and I will never be able to forgive you. You are a piece of crap! You only confessed because I had you like a rat in a trap."

"Listen, Blake." I knew I had messed everything up with the lies, yet still hungered for his forgiveness. "I'm sorry for not coming clean. I just didn't want to hurt you and start telling tales about someone you love. Like I say, I wanted her—urged her—to sort her own mess out with you and not involve me."

"Well, I didn't even have what you call a mess till you showed up again in our lives."

He sounded so defeated.

"Blake. This wasn't planned. You have to believe me. Chloe is her own person. What would you want me to do—send her away, not even knowing why she'd come? Maybe she needed help. I didn't know, Blake. If I don't help your wife who is at the door begging to be let in, then I'm not standing by you either. But it wasn't my place to upset you and stir up your marriage. Chloe needs to sort herself out. It wasn't for me to get in the middle of you two."

"Well, you have."

I had given it my best, had genuinely pleaded.

Blake might not have been the nicest recently, but he had been a good friend, and I couldn't bear the thoughts of losing him over my own moment of weakness. Not that I'd done a thing.

"How could you do this to me?" I could feel the pain in his voice as I stared across at the TV, which was coincidentally playing a scene of the movie, The Best Man, where Morris Chestnut found out his best friend had slept with his bride to be.

If this wasn't a sign that the universe was against me, I wondered what was.

"You know the worst thing…" His voice was suddenly calm, as though he had not even been crying a few seconds ago. "…you had her, but karma is a mother…, TB. Your day is coming."

"But you got it all wrong!" I tried to explain, but he wasn't willing to hear it. "I never did 'have her' as you say. I let her in, listened to her talk. That's it. She fell asleep."

"Put my wife on the phone. Now."

"Listen to me, Blake…"

"Put my wife on the phone before I come over there and blow your brains out, you no good bastard." He yelled and cussed in a way I hadn't heard him yell and cuss before.

"Help me, God," I said in a whisper, getting up and heading for the bedroom.

Pushing the bedroom door open, my eyes met with Chloe's, who was sitting up on the bed, watching the movie Acrimony.

"It's Blake," I said bluntly, dropping the phone on the foot of the bed. I walked out of the room feeling like the scum of the earth. Grabbing the last Corona, I headed into the living room at a turtle's pace. It was 1:24 a.m.

Halfway through the Corona, soft footsteps approached the living room. My attention turned to the entranceway.

"It's for you," Chloe whispered, tearfully handing me the phone. "A call just came in for you after I spoke to Blake. Anyway, I did explain everything to Blake. I told him it wasn't your fault. Just give him some time and he'll forgive you."

I took the handset off her but never spoke to see who the caller was. It wasn't Blake and that, at least, was some relief. "Forgive me? Forgive me for what exactly? I didn't even do a thing in all this mess you caused." The words bounced recklessly in my brain as I shook my head, not wanting to believe this was really happening, but it was.

"None of this is my fault…" I said through clenched teeth, chugging down the beer in my grip, "You were the one who showed up to my house unannounced and now my friendship with Blake is over because of it. How can this be happening?"

"I told you it wasn't over. That he'll forgive you. Anyway, haven't you ever read the Bible story about Cain and Abel?" She was kneeling in front of me, then reached to stroke the side of my face with her hand. "All right then. If you want me to be more open, I will be. Blake hates you Todd, and me being here has nothing to do with it. The sooner you realize this, the better off you'll be. I'm sorry you had to find out this way, but sometimes, the truth hurts. What I said he'd forgive you for doesn't have a lot to do with tonight. In fact, not anything to do with it."

"What do you mean he hates me?" I stared blankly at her. She was trying to remove the bottle of Corona from my grip and place it on the table.

"Open your eyes, Todd." She kissed me on the cheek. "He wants to be you. He's jealous."

"But why?" I whispered, trying to recollect his every uncalled bitterness toward me. "He has everything a man could ever want in life. Doesn't he?"

"He doesn't have my heart..." she said.

For someone whose husband had just caught her red-handed with her ex, her voice was extremely cold, rid of any form of guilt or pity for innocent Blake. "You do have my heart."

Standing up from her kneeling position, she turned on her heels as she crossed through the living room doorway. Stopping abruptly, she turned.

"Don't forget, your brother Khalil's on the phone."

Chapter 30

"MAYBE YOU SHOULD consider finding new friends." Khalil was laughing, having gotten abreast of the situation. He'd also shown up unannounced at my front door, as late as it was. Chloe was still here too, seeming more reluctant than ever to get her coat on and go back home to the man she was supposed to be with. She swore she'd explained everything to Blake, and it was all okay.

Or it was okay for her, anyway. But right now, I had Khalil to entertain and had to put my issues with Blake to one side for a while. Khalil had been out for a few beers and was still a live wire, full of energy and still not ready to call it a night. Dropping in on his brother at almost 2 a.m. must have seemed a great idea, probably looking to raid my usually stocked refrigerator.

"I tried to warn you about that snake Blake, but your stubborn ass didn't want to listen. For the last time, don't trust him. Will you actually hear me this time or ignore me again?"

I still hadn't been able to figure out exactly what Khalil knew about Blake, but considering he had zero friends, I found it annoying that he thought he could offer advice about finding new friends without taking the advice himself. He had to *find* some friends to begin with! At least I had one. Or I had had one. It was unclear what the situation with Blake now would be.

"Oh, he's all right," I heard my own pathetic voice arguing despite my better self. God only knew why, after everything. "Blake's a ride-or-die kind of friend and someone I trust with my life." I said, as though I was presenting my closing argument to a jury of twelve.

"If there's one person I can count on to be there for me, it's Blake." I added that with a tone of finality, trying to convince myself that Blake was everything I said he was.

Who was I fooling, really?

Maybe I just didn't like the fact that Khalil judged Blake, even when he didn't even know him; it just didn't seem fair. How could any person judge a stranger that way? It was a human flaw, the urge to put people down. It wasn't one of the best parts of humankind in my view.

"I know what you're thinking…" He jerked his head around, staring right at me, "…You're sitting over there thinking I don't know what I'm talking about, right?"

"Mmm-hmm." I nodded. "And you may be right."

"Well…" He exhaled a long breath, tapping his index finger on his lips, probably contemplating if he should give them the permission to say what they wanted. "Let's just say your best friend, Blake, is the reason I was sent to juvie."

"What?" I shouted, my eyeballs almost bulging out of their sockets. "You've got to be kidding me." I chuckled uneasily. "What, really?"

"I think it's time that you know everything about your long-lost twin brother Khalil."

He sat up straight on the couch adjacent to me as I waited with bated breath to hear Khalil's side of this story. Having discovered we were brothers over a year ago, he had, however, remained tight-lipped about his life, and I barely knew enough about him to make him more than any other stranger on the street. Now he was hitting me with this all of a sudden?

"It was a Tuesday morning on one of the last days of summer. The sun was just peeking over the horizon, staining the pale morning sky with orange streaks," he started, laughing at his own choice of descriptive words. I chuckled softly, hoping he didn't change his mind about talking.

"I had barely opened my eyes, staring blankly out the window at the painted sky, when the only person I trusted at the group home, my boy Sanchez Howard stormed in.

"'Get up and get dressed! Those punks who challenged us the other day are out back,' he shouted, grabbing my shoulders, as he shook me roughly. I quickly pushed him away, swinging my legs over the edge of the bed as I sat up. 'How long have they been waiting?'

"'I don't know! Just get dressed,' he said, and he was pacing restlessly.

"So, 'Give me ten minutes,' I'd said back, motioning for him to sit and calm himself down."

Khalil looked over at me.

I stared back, urging him with my eyes to go on with his narration.

"Well, every story should start from the beginning, right?"

He looked at me, wide eyed. I nodded in the affirmative.

"This particular story starts with my recent arrival at the House of Hope Group Home. I'd decided to keep mainly to myself, knowing it was a long way from the place I'd been calling home before then! Before getting kicked out by my so-called 'family', I'd learnt it was better to play my cards close to my chest. Being in inner city Boston, most guys were either dealers or thugs already up to their necks in criminal activity. Sanchez, one of the older kids who'd been at the home for a while, was the only one to try getting to know me, though I was cautious and made sure anything shared with him was insignificant. I wasn't the type to trust anyone. Not in those days. It had gotten me in trouble before, making me realize that trusting only made you vulnerable. Now, let's head back to Tuesday morning."

Well, I had to hand it to Khalil, he was good with his words.

"A few minutes later, we, I mean Sanchez and I, were headed out the door, toward the blacktop out back. I heard our challengers, Leon Pollack and Bryce Taylor, before I saw them, flinging insults and bragging about how they were going to destroy us.

"Leon, who was tall, burly, and always smelled like expired lunch meat, was constantly walking around our group home as though he owned it. And his counterpart, Bryce, was short, stocky and much lighter-skinned than Leon, with dirty dreadlocks that looked like they hadn't been washed in years. Rumor had it he was the best baller in the group home, but he had never gone up against me before. In fact, no one at the group home had ever seen me ball.

"Well, only Sanchez had. Impressed with my basketball skill, he made me an offer I couldn't refuse; he'd actually give me a pair of his Air Jordans if I teamed up with him to beat Leon and Bryce! You can well imagine what that meant to a kid who had next to nothing and was living in social care. It was like saying he'd give me five hundred bucks. I'd always wanted a pair of Air Jordans and he had about five—no kidding—so I agreed! What else would I do? The only condition attached to this deal of ours was simple: I'd only get the Jordans if we won.

"With the ball in play, the game began to roll fast, with Leon and Bryce scoring first.

"Leon was celebrating Bryce's latest score, whooping and hollering, but I evened it for us just moments later. For the next twelve points, our game went back and forth like that, tying up again. But toward the end, I once again stole the ball from Leon and made a layup.

"So I said, 'Let's stop joking around and finish them off. And when we win, don't forget I want those Retro Jordans!' Sanchez replied with a grin and a nod, and we jogged down the court.

"With this new focus, we took our game up a notch. Even though it was our first time on the court together, it was as if Sanchez and I had teamed up loads of times because honestly, every pass was perfect, and we sank every shot! In no time, we were winning twenty to twelve.

"Probably sensing imminent defeat, Leon began to take the dirty route. As I dribbled past him, he swung his elbow at my face but I stepped back, and he missed!

"'Watch your elbow!' I shouted at him.

"'Whatever!' he shouted back.

"'Yeah, well, throw another elbow and let's see what happens.' As you can imagine, I immediately regretted the threats I'd chucked at him, but there was no way back. It was just a heat of the moment thing. And I'd been feeling kind of invincible.

"I hadn't been at the group home very long back then, but I'd already heard about Leon's insanely short temper on the first day. As soon as the words were out of my mouth, Leon immediately dropped the ball and charged me. He'd been in plenty of fights and knew exactly where he was aiming, though it wasn't my first fight, either. At the last second, I stepped aside, taking him in with a heavy right hook. He went down! Slammed the ground like a jackhammer.

"So, I was looking down at him, hoping he'd have the good sense to stay down, but he didn't. He popped right back up in a fighting stance. Without waiting to catch his breath, he charged at me again and then we were suddenly surrounded, the crowd cheering. I mean, these kids loved a fist fight. It must have made their week seeing us going at each other like that!

"So anyway, I sidestepped him again and again, managing to get in a few heavy blows every time, so focused, I only vaguely noticed when all those onlookers parted to let some short, fat kid with bulbous protruding eyes stride toward us. 'Get off of him before I kill you!' he shouted, grabbing the back of my shirt, and flinging me across the court because he caught me unaware.

"That fat kid was far stronger than he looked because my body did a double barrel roll before I got my feet back under me! I turned to face my new attacker, tightening my fists and charging at him, managing to get an uppercut to his flabby chin. Think you could say he wasn't quite prepared for my intense assault, and he dropped to his knees, curling into a fetal position with his arms over his face. I wasn't done yet, letting fly blow after blow, pummeling every unprotected part of him as the watching crowd of kids screamed and punched the air, urging me on.

"There was so much adrenaline coursing through me that I never even saw the staff members rushing forward to break up the fight. About five of them. Before I knew it, someone's strong hands were pinning my arms behind me, pulling me from the blacktop."

Khalil sighed, catching his breath from all the talking. He was pumped up too.

"Two hours later, I was on a hard, armless chair outside the office of Mr. Tannerhill, the director of the group home. It was obviously bad news to be called into the director's office.

"After a while of waiting, Mr. Tannerhill came out, slamming his heavy door behind him to make more impact. It worked, and I'll never forget that grim look plastered on his face. Seething, he was. And he looked at me square in the eyes and said, 'We're ready for you, Khalil.'

"Already aware of the trouble I'd just got myself into as I stood up to follow him into his office, he turned and gave me an unexpected fatherly hug. It was weird!

"'Everything is going to be fine,' he whispered, but his

reassurance felt off. Looking down at me, he took a deep breath and opened the office door, ushering me in.

"I couldn't possibly forget the small table in the corner of the office because a well-dressed, white woman was sitting with long, curly, red hair brushed around her face. She had this really kind smile and that was the first thing to strike me as I entered the office. But standing right next to her was some tall, stern guy in black cargo pants and a short-sleeved gray polo shirt.

"Mr. Tannerhill positioned himself behind his desk and let the red-haired woman greet me.

'Hi, Khalil. My name's Susan Yearly, and I'm the social worker assigned to your case.'

"'Case? What case?' This was bewildering. Where did a social worker come into this? But before she could reply, that really tall man pulled out silver handcuffs from behind his back.

"'I'm Officer Terry. You're under arrest for assaulting Leon Pollack and Blake Harden.'

"'Blake Harden? Who the hell's Blake Harden?' I asked. "Never even heard of him."

"'But no one answered; was that fat kid Blake?'

"Without wanting to hear my side of the story, this Officer Terry guy pulled my hands behind my back and snapped on the restraints—they hurt too—silently walking with me down the hallway, straight out through the front door. No sooner had I arrived than they had me out again!

The following morning, a couple of officers came, bundled me into a van and dragged me off to the Juvenile and Domestic Relations District Court, where the judge looked down his nose at me like I was scum and promptly sentenced me to five years inside the Massachusetts Juvenile Corrections Reform Center for Boys. I was thirteen years old, for Christ's sake. Thirteen!"

"It's no age," I agreed. "They weren't at all compassionate toward you. I'm sorry, bruh."

I didn't know what else to say. Khalil had been through hell on earth.

Well, at least a whole lot of things were clearer now as I stared at Khalil. He sure had been through a lot from a really young age. Somehow, it made me feel guilty for escaping it.

"During my time in juvie, I vowed to make sure Blake Harden paid for having me sent there. I just didn't know he would turn out to be the best friend of my twin brother, did I?"

The room was deathly silent, my eyes wandering toward the entranceway to see Chloe standing there with tears in her eyes. Hell. I'd forgotten all about her still being in my place!

What did she hear? Had she been standing there the entire time?

No doubt she had questions I couldn't really give an answer to. She wiped away tears on her face with the back of her right hand, before stepping forward to envelop Khalil in a hug.

Still seated on the couch, trying to wrap my mind around everything Khalil had shared, my phone screen lit up with a call. It was on silent to avoid distractions during Khalil's narration.

Reaching for the phone to see who the caller was, my heart stopped beating for half a second.

Not again! When will he stop calling?

The name *Blake* danced on the screen.

Chapter 31

IT WAS A FEW weeks after hearing Khalil's heart-wrenching testimony about Blake, and Jane was sitting with me in my office, celebrating the firm's insider trading victory.

Judy walked in, closing the door gently behind her.

"What are you up to?" I asked, seeing the smile tugging up one corner of her top lip as I opened the bottle of Dom Pérignon Blake had given me as a pre-wedding gift over a year ago.

My hand offered a filled glass to Jane.

"Why don't you join us?" I suggested, right away lifting a third glass from my cabinet.

Jane lifted her glass in midair before gulping down the contents. "Yes, join us, Judy!"

"I would love to…." She made her way over to the desk and leaned against it. "But your twin brother Khalil, and his friend just arrived. So I can't! And you can't have one either!" she said to me mischievously, looking over her shoulder at Jane with the grin of a little devil.

She'd deliberately added the 'twin brother' title.

"You're a twin?" Jane gasped, nearly choking on her drink, but all I could think of was getting an answer to why Khalil was here. Grabbing the neck of the expensive bubbly, I drank straight from the bottle, spilling a few drops on the lapel of my new suit in the process.

Closing my laptop, I dashed out of my office to find out for myself what Khalil was doing here. Jane and Judy followed close behind.

"Didn't even know Todd had a twin brother," I heard Jane whisper. "Are they identical?"

"Yes, girl," Judy's voice bellowed with excitement. "And he is *nothing* like Attorney Banks. He's bad to the bone. Just the way I like them." She spoke loudly, no doubt for me to hear it.

Turning on my heel to end their meaningless chatter ringing in my ears, Jane inadvertently slammed right into me, causing her to lose her balance. Reaching out, I gripped her by the hand and pulled her close, my other hand sliding around her waist, saving her from hitting the floor.

Everything suddenly seemed to be moving in slow motion, her hands on my pounding heart, staring down at her slightly parted lips and closed eyes.

Judy was still watching the scene unfold, my gaze falling on her iPhone pointed at us. I quickly let go of Jane's small waist, barely escaping the camera's flash.

"Attorney Banks!" Judy yelled, looking over Jane's shoulder. "You ruined my photo."

Finally making it to the lobby in one piece, I greeted Khalil, who was standing next to a taller gentleman resembling the actor Shemar Moore. He wore an uncomfortable smile.

"He is gorgeous!" Jane's voice broke out behind me, referring to Khalil, I presumed.

Her sudden outburst arrested any words I had for him. Next thing, she scurried right in front of me like a groupie willing to kill everyone in the way to reach a rock star.

"So you must be Todd's infamous twin brother?"

She did push me out of the way, flashing her widest smile at him, green eyes lighting up. She had a way of saying the most ridiculous things, but by using a certain teasing tone, every man fell at her feet, somehow unoffended and finding her perfectly wonderful. Even my brother seemed taken in by it. "I'm Attorney Jane Moore, and you are?" She stretched out her hand.

Khalil, obviously thrilled by the unexpected and unusual level of attention, chuckled softly.

"Khalil!" he said softly, taking her small hand in his. "And this is my friend, Sanchez."

So, this was presumably the same Sanchez as the one from the group home. What was he doing here with Khalil? This could not be good. Although of course, I accepted years had gone by and these were men now, not unruly kids. Still, there was an uneasy feeling and air between us. I found my eyes sizing up this Sanchez fellow as he deliberately avoided my gaze.

"It's nice to meet the two of you." Jane giggled, leaning forward as she stood on her toes, gripping Khalil's shoulders and kissing him on his cheek. She seemed a touch inebriated, though I was sure she had only had one glass of our bubbly. Some days, I wondered if she kept alcohol at work too, taking a secret little indulgence. She seemed to get drunk too easily otherwise.

"Break it up. Break it up." I stepped in between the two of them when I saw the firm's managing partner's office door open. We had been giving the impression of holding an office party.

This kind of thing could cause problems and was a bad example to younger, newer staff.

Quickly whizzing Khalil and Sanchez out of the lobby, we headed for my office before things got out of hand. Over my shoulder, however, I caught sight of Jane fanning herself with a hand.

Her lips were just mouthing the word, 'hot'.

It was impossible not to chuckle at her display of lustful attraction.

Closing the door to the office behind me, I pulled the string on the mini window blinds before walking behind my desk to take a seat.

"This is my boy, Sanchez. The one I told you about a few weeks ago," Khalil said, turning to Sanchez as I nodded in understanding. "And he needs your help."

Sanchez's sweaty face spoke volumes; it was as though he had seen a ghost on his way here.

"How can I help?"

"Okay," he exhaled heavily, adjusting himself on the chair. "How long does a cold case stay open for unsolved murders?"

"What do you mean, unsolved murders?" I turned to Khalil, who didn't seem affected by the question, but something told me there was more to this. *What was he involved with?* I thought.

"Ten years ago, someone broke into my uncle's home and killed him. The case went cold, but I think I may have evidence on who committed the crime. Can it be reopened?"

"Well, that depends on the jurisdiction and the crime. The statute of limitations is a legal principle that the passage of time makes it harder to provide a defense against a charge for a crime. Evidence can be lost. Records are thrown out and oftentimes, memories fade. Sometimes, people die or head off to unknown parts of the world. Without concrete evidence, the chance to charge anybody usually expires."

"So are you saying nothing can be done?"

He broke into a smile, his eyes squinting slightly. For someone who had evidence to pin his uncle's murderers, being happy wasn't an emotion he should have after my explanation.

"The good news is…" I got up from my chair, sitting on the edge of my desk. "Murder is an exception to the rule. Someone can be charged and tried for murder at any time for the rest of their life. If you define solvable as charging someone and having them found guilty in a court of law, then the statute of limitations dictates when the investigation should stop. By that definition, a person who dies before getting charged, even for murder, has gotten away with it, even if it is learned later that the person likely committed the crime."

"So what are you saying, Attorney Banks?"

He leaned forward, the smile fading from his face as his eyebrows drew together. He was obviously pissed by my round-about statements. But it was these round-about statements that contributed toward making me a good attorney.

"What I'm saying is this…" I was congratulating myself for confirming my initial thoughts, by just observing how he'd incriminated himself with his own emotions. "If your uncle's killer is still alive, the case is never closed. If the killer's deceased, the state's unlikely to investigate."

"That's what I was afraid of!"

He violently slammed his fist on the desk, storming out of my office.

Peering across the desk at Khalil, whose head was lowered, I swallowed hard.

"Who else knows?" I asked.

Chapter 32

LONDON WAS SCHEDULED to fly into Boston for the weekend, and I was happier than a pig at feeding time. The late nights working on the insider trader case with Jane had completely derailed our weekend visits. And with London working for the agency on a wall-sized painting of Chicago's Willis Tower Skydeck, the twelfth tallest building in the world, we rarely had time for each other outside of day-to-day phone calls and FaceTime.

Today promised to be a good day and I was excited to see her.

SECRETS ENEMY

Boston Logan International Airport was jammed with people and smells, and the traffic was thick and loud. London's flight wasn't scheduled to arrive until 4:00 p.m. I had an hour to kill.

Pulling up to the curb, I parked behind a bright red Chevy Suburban with New York plates. An older white man wearing a gray and blue Aaron Judge New York Yankees jersey was loading suitcases in the rear of the car, when he turned to me and began pumping his fist in the air.

"Go Yankees!" he shouted repeatedly, apparently forgetting he was in Red Sox nation.

I caught myself harboring a feeling of resentment toward him for calling out the name of our hated rival in the heart of Boston. Instead, I just smiled at him, connecting my Spotify playlist to the car. Jamming to Meek Mill's hit song, Going Bad, I spotted one of the city's finest headed my way. She wore dark sunglasses, a fitted Boston Police uniform, and an all-business attitude to match. Lowering the volume, my hands trembled as I placed them on the steering wheel. She motioned for me to roll the car window down, and I obliged quickly, tensing up as she got closer.

Why did we black men have such an unhealthy fear of the police?

They were hired to serve and protect law abiding citizens like me, so why was I shaking with fear? Afterall, we were supposed to be on the same side of the law, right?

"License and registration." She glared at me.

"My license is in my wallet and the registration's in the glove compartment. Permission to retrieve both?"

Kneeling, she dropped her hands on the door and poked her head inside the car to look around. Her breath was minty fresh. Looking through the rearview mirror, there was a large box of case files and a twelve pack of Corona on the backseat. "Permission to do both."

Taking a deep breath, I slowly removed my wallet from the inside pocket of my blazer and handed her my driver's license. Before I could open the glove compartment for the vehicle registration, she stepped away from the car, glancing at my license.

"You're that hotshot attorney, Todd Banks, aren't you?" A warm smile flashed across her hardened face, somehow softening it. "The one who sank the CEO from that large corporation?"

"Yes, Officer. Attorney Todd Banks."

"I knew it was you." She punched my arm playfully. "Our precinct loves your firm. Keep up the good work. And continue to put those bad guys in prison."

Where had I heard that before?

"Have a great day, Attorney Banks." She turned on her heels and headed the other way.

Relieved I wasn't caught on the wrong side of the law, I slumped down in my seat and grabbed my phone to change the song. I'd missed five calls from London. I paused my playlist, not bothering to listen to London's voicemails, calling her instead.

The phone rang several times before she answered.

"Hey," I lowered the stereo volume. "I didn't see that you called. Are you okay?"

I was concerned.

"Spotify again?" she joked. "I'm safe, but my flight was canceled. Supposedly, a winter storm is brewing, canceling all flights. Trust me to pick exactly this timing."

"Come on, baby, I—"

London cut me off. "I wanted nothing more than to make it back to you!"

"Listen." I sighed heavily and leaned forward. "It's not your fault. We'll figure this out."

"I'm just ready to come home, baby." Her voice was relatively calm for someone who was obviously frustrated. "Did you know, I almost didn't take the project to paint the mural? But I couldn't pass it up. It was a once-in-a-lifetime opportunity.

An opportunity that will put me in the ranks of some of the best artists we have today."

"You are one of the best," I reassured her. "And you've already taken the world by storm. Your best is yet to come. And if you don't already know, I'm your biggest fan."

"I'm glad that you're supportive of me and what I do. But missing you is another animal! I don't think I can take another week of only phone and video calls. It doesn't compare to being in your presence. And I know you've been working late nights to win the high-profile case, and I hoped to celebrate with you this weekend, no thanks to American Airlines."

"Well, we're going to figure this out." I tried to switch the phone to FaceTime, but she didn't answer. "Is everything okay? I'm trying to FaceTime you."

"Yes, everything is fine, sweetheart." Her voice was unusually quiet, which only meant she had a lot on her mind. "I will happily FaceTime you when I get out of this zoo called an airport. I'll call when I get back in the car. Love you!"

"Love you too, baby!"

We hung up.

Chapter 33

KHALIL AND I were hanging out at the Violet Lounge, knocking back Bacardi shots when Blake and Chloe walked in looking every bit like celebrities.

"Isn't that your boy Blake and the pastor from the church?" He tipped his shot glass back and drained it. "What are they doing here together?"

As I watched the two of them saunter into the VIP room, it suddenly dawned on me that I hadn't shared the news about their sudden nuptials with Khalil.

"Bartender?" I called out, nervously rubbing the top of my legs with my palms.

But it was true. What were they doing here? And of all nights, why tonight?

As I tried to conjure a way to tell Khalil they were married without looking like a fool, the bartender arrived. "Another shot?"

"Make it a double."

As quickly as he filled the shot glass, I downed it. Turning to Khalil, I winced. "They're married." My voice was almost monotone.

"Get the hell out of here!" He slapped the back of my neck. "There's no way she would knowingly marry that snake. I thought Kevin Hart was funny. You got jokes, baby bruh."

Khalil was right. What would possess Chloe to marry someone who didn't have a committed bone in his body? Maybe this was their way of paying me back for leaving her standing at the altar.

"It's true."

"I'll find out for myself." He slipped off his motorcycle jacket and black Timberland boots, handing me both. "Give me your blazer and those corny ass loafers, will you?"

"How are you gonna do that?" I began untying my shoes, staring up at him suspiciously.

"We're identical twins, bruh." He slipped on my blazers and shoes. Tipping back his shot, he turned and smiled devilishly at me. "I'll be right back."

Making his way through the crowd, he headed straight for the VIP room, where Blake unhooked the velvet rope and invited him in.

I shook my head in wonder as the bartender filled my shot glass and gave me the thumbs up. "On the house." He looked over my shoulder. "And for your friend?"

I slowly turned on the barstool, and there before me stood a gorgeous brown-skinned woman with thick curly hair and full lips. It was Nicole, Khalil's lady friend.

"I'll have an Amaretto sour." She kissed me on the back of the neck and then joined me at the bar. "I'm sorry I'm late, but interstate 93 traffic was a nightmare. Have you been waiting long? Where's Todd?"

Wow, did Khalil and I look that much alike? Maybe it was the Timberland boots and motorcycle jacket that threw her off. Either way, our shared face was both a blessing and a curse.

"It's me, Todd." I said with a joyous expression, but the puzzled look in her eyes told me she didn't believe me.

"Khalil." She grabbed her drink from the bar and took a

sip. "Todd wears loafers and blazers. He doesn't have your swag. He has swans!"

"Swans?" I chuckled. "What are swans?"

"Swans! The opposite of swag. Someone with absolutely no style. Todd may look like you, but those tight-fitted khakis and over-the-top wool blazers are a little white boyish, don't you think?"

Removing my wallet from my back pocket, I dropped my driver's license on the bar to prove to her once and for all I was not Khalil. Ignoring me, she got up from the bar and wrapped her arms around me in a bear hug, all but dragging me onto the dance floor when the song 'Too Close' by the group Next blared from the speakers.

"That my song," She moved her hips seductively from side to side and gently placed her hands on my shoulders, pulling me in for a full embrace.

"Is that a new cologne you're wearing?" She sighed and put her head on my chest. "I like it."

Oh, hell no. I released her and stepped away. This game of cat and mouse was going too far.

"I'm really Todd." I flashed my driver's license in her face. Peering down at the small letters on the plastic card, she immediately walked off the dance floor, shaking her head.

"Did Khalil put you up to this?"

"I tried to tell you earlier, but all you talked about was me not having any swag. And who says swans, anyway?"

At once, she burst out laughing.

"You have to admit, that was funny, and you really need to retire the loafers and blazer look."

"But I like my loafers and blazers." I smiled, and then filled her in on what Khalil was up to.

"Wait a minute." She spun on the barstool to face me. "You're telling me that your best friend married your ex and didn't even invite you to the wedding? What kind of reality show BS is this? I'm being punked, aren't I? Where is Ashton Kutcher?"

Grabbing her drink from the bar, she looked me square in the eyes and laughed hysterically, as if the two of them being married was some kind of joke. Or maybe she was laughing at me, and I was the joke. It wouldn't be the first time in my life if so.

"It's cool." I gulped down my shot and peered over her shoulder toward the VIP room, where Khalil, Blake and Chloe walked out.

Nicole was still laughing when I got up from the bar and wrapped my arms around her neck. "They're heading our way. Remember, pretend I'm Khalil, okay?"

It took everything in her not to laugh in my face, but she swallowed hard and agreed.

"I got you."

Moments later, they arrived.

"You remember my brother, right?" Khalil said to Blake and Chloe, smiling at Nicole and me.

"How could I forget the second half of the infamous Doublemint twins?"

After introducing Nicole, Chloe invited us to join them in the VIP room. We sauntered through the crowd, and Khalil hooked his arm around my neck.

Leaning in, he whispered. "Why is Chloe telling me she's in love with me and ready to leave Blake? You have a lot of explaining to do, bruh."

Chapter 34

I WAS SITTING at the bar in the VIP room, sipping on a Corona and watching Chloe, Blake, Khalil and Nicole laughing it up at the table a few feet away.

Blake and Chloe had no idea Khalil was putting on the performance of a lifetime, being me. He was so convincing that he almost fooled me too.

"Can I get another Corona?" I flagged down the female bartender with the long black hair and killer bod. She shot me a perfect smile, placing a black shot glass on the bar in front of me. She filled it with a brown liquor with which I was unfamiliar.

Leaning forward, she whispered, "This is a very strong drink, so proceed with caution."

Grabbing the drink from the bar, I downed it within a second, but it burned like hell. "What the hell is in this?" I coughed, almost bending double in discomfort, my gullet on fire.

"I told you to proceed with caution."

She filled a shot glass for herself and chugged it. "Ahhhhh! This Stroh 160 Rum is fire. It will burn a hole in your soul. My name is Kayla." She extended her hand for a formal greeting. "And you are?"

"It's nice to meet you, Kayla." I grabbed her finely manicured hand. "Todd. Todd Banks."

Stepping away from the bar, she looked at me confused.

"If you are Todd Banks, then who is that over there?" She pointed toward the table where Khalil was sitting.

"That's my twin brother Khalil," I said. "He's pretending to be me."

"Wait." She leaned in a second time. "Why would he do that?"

"Well," I took a deep breath. "The gorgeous light-skinned woman with long hair used to be my fiancée, but a few months ago, she married the guy in the black suit. He is my best friend." I knew it was alcohol talking, but I wouldn't shut up. "I told my brother they were married but he didn't believe me, so we swapped clothes for him to find out."

"Wait a minute." She tipped the bottle back and gulped. "Your best friend married your ex-fiancée? What in the jiminy crickets is going on here? Just when I thought I'd seen everything. A reality show is going down inside the Violet Lounge, and on my shift. What are the odds and where the hell are the cameras?"

She swooped from behind the bar and began looking for hidden cameras.

"This is not a reality show," I laughed out loud. "And there are no cameras."

Grabbing the bottle from the bar, I headed toward the exit. I had had enough.

****

Being an identical twin was a blessing and a curse. Unless one of the twins had a known physical difference, it was nearly impossible to tell who was who between the pair of us.

Since discovering Khalil was my twin brother over a year ago, he'd always kept it real with me, and I didn't take him for someone who'd betray me. But then I remembered Blake telling me something. According to Blake, it was written in the Bible that a person's worst enemy would be a member of his own family. So if it was written in the Holy Scriptures, it had to be true, right?

I was stuck at a crossroad with nowhere to turn, and no one to trust.

I was sprawled out on the couch enjoying a bag of popcorn and watching TV when I heard a knock at the door. Who could have the audacity to interrupt my chill time at this hour?

Tiptoeing toward the door, I peered through the peephole.

No freaking way! Not again!

What was Chloe doing here and why did she think it was okay to show up to my house without calling first? After the last time, you'd have thought she might have learned her lesson. But no, she evidently had not. Well, I was going to teach her a thing or two about etiquette.

By now, I was sick and tired of being disrespected; it was time to draw the line in the sand once and for all, even if it meant losing my friendship with her.

Taking a deep breath, I slowly turned the doorknob and opened the door.

"Hey." In what appeared to be a return of the last unpleasant and uninvited encounter, she lowered her head and angrily pushed past me, beelining straight into the living room. With her arms folded across her chest, she plopped down on the couch and stared coldly at me.

"You are not funny, Todd."

"What are you talking about?" I stood in the living room entrance, still upset about her unannounced visit.

I'd had enough.

"Listen, Chloe." I sat across from her, elbows on my knees, watching her. "How would you feel if I stormed into one of your private church meetings, or stopped by your home in the middle of the night while you and Blake were sleeping? Being a pastor doesn't give you the right to show up at my home unannounced. With all due respect, it's quite rude."

She stared at me shockingly, as if I was speaking a foreign language. But for me, the rubber was finally meeting the road. I was putting my foot down, dammit.

As tough as I sounded or appeared, however, she had me mesmerized by her stunning beauty. Her coke bottle figure and perfect skin had me panting like a deer for water tonight.

Snap out of it, Todd, I heard a small voice call out. *The flesh is weak. Don't give into it. Run.*

Run? Where the hell was I running to? This was my house. Ignoring the still small voice, I stared at her lustfully, ready to pounce and devour her. But betraying London was not an option, even if my body was trying to deceive me. I would not betray London. I seriously loved her.

Getting up from the couch, I dashed into the kitchen for a cool drink before things got out of control. Grabbing a chilled water out of the refrigerator, I heard her soft voice.

She was inches from my face when I turned.

"Since we're being honest…" She dropped her hands on my shoulders, leaned forward and whispered. "I didn't think it was cool or funny how your twin tried pretending to be you the other night. It was outright childish. But that's neither here nor there."

Reaching up, she wrapped her arms around my neck, closed her eyes and puckered up.

"I love you, Todd Banks. Kiss me."

HUNTER'S
FINALE

Chapter 35

AUNT JANE WAS still sound asleep on the couch when I casually strolled into the house, feeling as if I had just scored the winning basket to lead Cloud Valley High to the Massachusetts basketball state championship. Kissing Destiny for the first time had been far more than I could have imagined. Her lips were rose petal soft, her breath sweeter than Aunt Jane's pumpkin pie.

Despite being roughed up by her uncle earlier in the evening, and almost peeing on myself, it had all been worth it. I felt as if cupid had struck me with one of his teenage love arrows and Destiny's name was written all over it.

Right now, I was happier than a trick or treater with a basketful of their favorite candy.

I sauntered down the hall to check on Uncle Lee, and to thank him for allowing me to borrow his truck to drive Destiny home. It was the perfect end to the day, especially since crazy Harper decided to crash the dinner party. And why would Aunt Jane think it was a good idea to invite her without first consulting me, anyway? What was she up to?

Uncle Lee's bedroom door was partly open when I poked my head inside. He was sprawled across the bed as per usual, sipping on a beer and watching the end of the Celtics game when my phone vibrated in my pocket, breaking my concentration.

The call came from a private number. No doubt it was Harper since she'd threatened to call me if she hadn't heard from me before midnight. Instead of letting the call go to voicemail to piss her off, I found myself reluctantly answering.

"Harper?" My voice was seemingly quiet as I headed out to the patio, plopped down on the wicker chair and kicked my feet up on the glass table.

"Who the hell is Harper?" a deep but eerie voice came through the phone. "I'm looking for Hunter. Is this him?"

"Who's asking?" I shot back like the neighborhood bully, but the tone of my voice was more like a frightened teenage girl at a horror movie than a leather coat-wearing tough guy.

"You don't remember me, do you?" He chuckled a sinister sound. "After all of these years, I finally found you and in my neck of the woods as well. What are the chances?"

"You must have confused me with someone else. No idea who you are." I put the phone on the table and hit the speaker button.

"Oh no," I heard him say. "I could never forget you, Hunter James. I'm going to finish the job I should have finished ten years ago."

"I know who this is," I said.

The line went dead.

My heart slammed against my rib cage, my veins cold, a sweat gathering on my forehead and all the way down my back, vomit rising into my throat. My vision was giving way to a dizzy blackness, and I leaned forward to put my head between my knees, faint.

Next, I was tumbling forward out of the patio chair.

On the ground, the phone was still by me. It took me back to that fateful night ten years ago. Mentally paralyzed for a brief moment, I looked up.

Aunt Jane was standing in the doorway with a terrified look.

"What did you hear?"

"Everything!"

With tears in my eyes, I said, "I think I know who killed my family."

TODD'S
FINALE

Chapter 36

WHEN I ARRIVED at the office the next morning, Jane could be seen sitting on the edge of her desk between two male figures seated on either side of her. Assuming they were clients, I headed straight into my office directly across from hers. No sooner had I popped the lid on my coffee, was Jane was standing in the doorway, distinctly troubled. She looked fearful, in fact.

"Good morning, Attorney Banks." She sauntered into my office and closed the door. It was the first time she'd ever called me Attorney Banks aloud. Her breath was barely above a whisper.

This couldn't be good.

"The older gentleman in my office is my husband, and the kid is my nephew." She plopped herself down in the chair in front of my desk. "I'm sure you've heard of him. Hunter James?"

"The name sounds vaguely familiar." My gaze searched her face for the answer, but there was nothing. "Why would I know him?"

"He's Cloud Valley high school's leading scorer. And is ranked the third best point guard in the country. He's been all over the news and has even appeared on SportsCenter."

"He's your nephew? Isn't he being recruited by every major college in the nation? Why didn't you tell me you were related to him?" Getting up from my desk and peering through the office window like a crazed fan, I laughed. "Goodness, Jane. You are a woman of secrets."

"Well, never mind that. We need your help, Todd. Hunter is in grave danger."

"Danger? What kind of danger?"

"Meet me in the conference room across from Judy's office in five minutes and we'll tell you everything."

Getting up from the chair, she turned and walked out.

Moments later, she was back. "And bring your coffee. It could be a long stint."

By the conference room, Jane was posted in the doorway like a security guard at a nightclub. After closing the door, she walked around the table and sat down in the chair between her husband and nephew. "This is my colleague, Attorney Todd Banks. One of the best criminal defense attorneys in the state of Massachusetts." Curious eyes followed as I grabbed a seat directly in front of the three of them. "I asked Attorney Banks to join us today."

"So you are the one who's been spending all these late nights with my wife?" Her husband got up and walked around the table to drop his big hands on my shoulders. Leaning down, he whispered in my ear. "If I was a betting man, which I am not... But if I was..." He laughed a second time. "I'd think you and my lovely wife were having an affair."

"Ha! Good, because that's one bet you would have lost."

"Really?" he responded with a raised eyebrow.

"I'm not interested in married women," I whispered. "Especially bossy ass white women. No pun intended, sir!"

Without saying another word, he stood tall and returned to his seat.

"Will the two of you stop joking around so we can get to business?" Jane said.

"What's going on?" I peered over the table at the three of them. "And how can I help?"

"Hunter?" Jane rubbed the top of his hand softly. "Tell Attorney Banks what you told me."

"I think I know who killed my family."

"What do you mean killed your family? I looked over at Jane. "You never told me your nephew's family had been murdered?"

"Let him finish," she interrupted me. "Start from the beginning, honey."

****

HUNTER.

I told them everything, all the way through, detailing that heinous night and the torment those two men delivered upon my family and me. Then I came to the end part… a part I'd never even told to Destiny. After they killed Dad and I saw his body slump, one went to wash blood off his hands at the sink. Then he said, "That's it, then. Let's get out of here, boss."

"No," the head henchman replied. "We can't leave yet." He sat on the chaise lounge, perusing our family photos on the end table. "The job's not done," he added. "More to do yet."

"What are you talking about?" The sidekick panicked. "The police will be here any minute."

SECRETS ENEMY

"This picture. Look at it." The boss man pointed. "What do you see? Look hard at it. It's not rocket science. Can you add up numbers?"

"It's the family we just killed. So what? And yes, I can add up numbers."

"Look at the picture again, you idiot. How many people are in this picture? And how many bodies do you see in this room?" He waved his gun between the picture and my dead family.

"Oh no. We missed one? So where's that other boy?"

****

TODD.

"I was the little boy who got away," Hunter said, tears streaming down his face. The boy was an absolute mess. "And I believe one of them is related to my friend. She'll be here any minute."

Wiping my brow with my hand, I felt the bile rise in my throat as anger began to take over.

Slamming my fist down on the table, I looked at Hunter. "I promise to make the people responsible for taking your family's lives pay. You have my word."

Just then, there was a knock on the conference room door. It was Judy.

"Your guest is here."

Hunter's eyes lit up as he darted out of the conference room. Moments later, he was back.

Turning in my chair, I couldn't believe my eyes.

"Destiny?" I called out.

"Uncle Todd?" she responded.

"What are you doing here?"

Printed in the USA
CPSIA information can be obtained
at www.ICGtesting.com
LVHW090942060524
778956LV00007B/7